CONVERSION ROAD

By John J. Weigand

ISBN 0-940169-10-X

Printed in the United States of America

Dedications

To my parents Edward and Margaret, my first teachers, whose love for God flowed out to every person they ever met. I'm forever grateful for their Love & for introducing me to a personable Jesus.

To my brother, Joe, and sisters, Mary Ann and Maria, who were students of the same school and have been a source of support to me in all that I've done.

To those men and women, my friends, who have taken their time to share with me their trip down Conversion Road. I thank them for their trust. It is because of their trust in me that I have a deeper relationship with Him.

To those men & women, my friends, who have listened to the stories contained in this book, and who encouraged and insisted that I write them down. It is because of their insistence that this book came to be.

To those who typed this manuscript, and drew the cover which has been revised and rewritten so many times. Their patience with me has been very edifying.

Introduction

CONVERSION ROAD

By John J. Weigand

When I want a spiritual book, I generally employ a four-step approach. The first step is to go to my favorite little Christian bookstore. My second step is to look for a title that catches my eye, and the third is to scan the table of contents to catch the chapter titles.

If your approach is similar, I'm sure you were puzzled when you read the table of contents of *Conversion Road*. After all, what does conversion have to do with a Peter or a John, or for that matter, even a centurion or a rich young man? And if you found it difficult to understand why these four men would be contained in such a book, you no doubt were completely befuddled when you found that the story of Judas was also contained here. This is precisely what a friend said when I told him of my title and the cast of characters to be found in the manuscript. You see, my friend and I had different definitions of 'conversion', and I remember clarifying mine by relating an incident of some fifteen years ago. Stationed as an associate in a parish, part of my responsibilities was to cover a small hospital not far from the parish house. About three o'clock one morning, I received a call from a nurse, saying there was a sweet little 84-year-old woman who was dying and really needed to see a priest. Before entering her room, I discovered that she had already been anointed, and I wondered why she had such a need to see me. I went in and there she was, sitting up, and she said, "Father, I just have to have this question answered." I smiled and asked, "What's the question?" And she said, "Can a Protestant make a good convert to Catholicism?"

She could see my puzzled expression so she went on to

explain. It seemed that her granddaughter had been in to visit her earlier that evening and had shared with her the fact that, before the marriage between herself and her fiancé was to take place, her fiancé was going to convert to Catholicism, and she just had to know whether converts could be good Catholics. I smiled at the old lady and said, "Yes, they can, and in fact, Catholics make good converts, too." I shouldn't have said that, because I was sure that now she was more puzzled than ever.

But what I meant by that statement was that, so often, we confuse the word "conversion" with the process of taking instructions and changing from one faith to another. That can be part of conversion but it surely isn't the complete definition. Conversion does not happen to an individual because he's part of an RCIA program. Conversion does not happen in a renewal weekend or a week-long mission in a parish. It does not even happen during a Sunday liturgy. This is not to say that conversion does not begin or is not helped on its way by the above. But conversion is not an event, it's a process. A process of life in relationship with God. Conversion is a journey. This conversion journey demands an openness to another person, a continuous striving to work at relationship. All of us need conversion, for we have all been created in the image and the likeness of God, yet there are certain things that hold us back from being that perfect image. Those little things in our lives that are signs of imperfection, those things that prevent us from being the best we can be.

The characters in this little book are individuals who came to realize their own imperfections and their need to walk down conversion road with a man called Jesus. The first that you will encounter is Augustus, the centurion. I've always wondered what it would have been like to be a bystander on that Good Friday, watching Jesus take the cross upon His shoulders and make His way to Calvary. And what better person to be that bystander than someone who was very close to Him on that journey? What better man than Augustus, the centurion? In a way, I envy Augustus. He was not prejudiced about the events that were unfolding. He was there, neither as a member of the crowd applauding these events, nor as one who hoped that it was just a bad dream. Augustus had no preconceived notions of who Jesus was, or what He should do. He had the unique opportunity of meeting Jesus just as He was. And what a beautiful, special moment it must have been for him.

The second person in my cast of characters who traveled down conversion road with Jesus is Peter, my favorite saint. It seems, sometimes, that all the books about saints would have us believe that they were perfect. Peter, on the other hand, is not depicted in the Scriptures as perfect. He is a paradox, at one and the same time strong in stature and in faith, yet beleaguered with weaknesses. As he journeyed down that conversion road with Jesus, he came to recognize his weaknesses and he began to deal with them. As a result, he is probably one of the greatest examples ever to walk down conversion road, to lead us on our pilgrim way to the Kingdom.

My third character is John, chosen partly because he is my namesake, and partly because, in a way, the story of John is the story of John Weigand. John's example has helped me to walk that road with Jesus as he did.

The next character is Tobias, the rich young man. I'm not entirely sure why I picked Tobias. Perhaps because I always wondered what happened to that young man after he had turned down the call of Jesus; perhaps because he reminds me that I encounter Jesus every day of my life. Not just in that personal call that Jesus gave to Tobias, but in and through the people in my life. The rich young man came to encounter Christ not only in the call that Jesus gave him, but also through the persons of Zacheus and of Paul.

My final character is Judas. As I stated earlier, you might question why the story of Judas would be contained in such a book. It seems to me that there are two questions here. The first question would be, why did I choose to tell the story of Judas? The second question would be, how could I include his story in a book called *Conversion Road*?

The first question could be answered by sharing with you

something my Spiritual Director told me many years ago. I had shared with him that someone close to me had really hurt me. He could tell how much it was affecting me. He told me what he always did when someone had hurt him. He claimed he would force himself to come up with five reasons why that person acted as he had. The first reason, he said, was usually the most uncharitable reason. The second reason was a little less uncharitable, because he had thought of the most uncharitable reason first. By the time he had reached the fifth reason, he found it was almost always a charitable reason. And it was the fifth reason he always chose to answer his question "why." He said some people count to ten, but if you do that, he said, you still haven't answered the question "why."

I decided to use my Spiritual Director's method in trying to discern for myself why Judas did what he did. I have always felt, because we know what Judas did, we always seemed to attribute the most uncharitable reason to why he did it. In using my Spiritual Director's method of dealing with hurts caused, I am not suggesting I know for sure why Judas did what he did. What is contained in this book about Judas are my thoughts and attempts to get under the skin of this man: to give him the benefit of the doubt, to learn from him in his strengths and in his weaknesses.

The second question concerning his inclusion in a book about conversion — well you'll just have to read his story to find that answer.

I shared with you at the beginning of this introduction that there are four steps I take in selecting a book. I have shared with you the first three steps: going to the store, looking for a catchy title, and reading the table of contents. The fourth step is reading the introduction. If I've been intrigued by the title and the table of contents, I usually try to read at least part of the introduction, to see if I really want to invest in that book. Since you've gotten this far into my introduction, I hope that you will be sufficiently enticed to continue.

Meditating about these five individuals has helped me to

recognize my need to walk with Jesus, to recognize my strengths and to deal with my weaknesses. I hope and pray that this little book will help you, too, in your journey with Jesus.

AUTHOR'S NOTE

When we look at the history of man, we tend to pick out individuals who have influenced that history and call them "heroes". We place these heroes on pedestals so high that they become unapprochable. All we can do with these heroes is to stand in awe of them.

Conversion Road is an attempt to make these heroes real. It is an attempt to make them human and approachable. When you read the pages of *Conversion Road,* you'll not find the recounting of the many miracles of Jesus. The Jesus depicted in these pages is a kind, gentle, loving, accepting and forgiving man who has come to share His Father's love: a Jesus who doesn't want you to stand in awe of Him but rather to stand in friendship with Him. When you read the pages of *Conversion Road* you'll not find the instant saintliness of a Peter or a John. The Peter and John depicted in these pages are rugged men struggling with their own identities and plagued with self-doubt and imperfections. Their saintliness comes only because they choose to accept Jesus' invitation to walk down Conversion Road with Him. They find that road hard but very fulfilling.

Of the five stories contained in *Conversion Road,* the first (The Centurion) is based on the Traditional fourteen Stations of the Cross; the second, third and fifth (Peter, John and Judas) are based on the scripture accounts of their lives and the fourth (Tobias, the Rich Young Man) has its roots in Scripture but blossomed in the author's imagination. It is the author's hope that listening to these men speak of their friendship with Jesus will help the reader to also accept Jesus' invitation to walk down Conversion Road with Him.

P.S. The author does wish anyone reading this book to know that, although the characters are based in Tradition and Scripture, it is solely his interpretation of these men, and not an attempt at exegesis.

Table of Contents

THE CENTURION

My name is Augustus. I am a Roman. My father is a member of the Roman Senate, having risen to power in and through the military. As his first son, I decided to follow in his footsteps. Currently I am assigned as a lieutenant of the guards in this God-forsaken place known as Jerusalem and am under the authority of a man called Pontius Pilate.

The events I am about to share with you concern my encounter with your friend Jesus. I have noted here my reflections, which cover the hours just before his death, so that you might come to know your friend from a slightly different perspective.

I must begin by telling you that I'm a person who doesn't believe in organized religion. God is just someone up there, if you have a need to believe in one. I don't have such a need.

My story really begins about three o'clock in the morning of that Friday when I first encountered Jesus. I had been summoned by Pilate to his palace. I came before him and was informed that a preacher by the name of Jesus had been arrested. Pilate was putting me in full charge of this Jesus until we had done what we had to do with him. I thought that this was rather strange. Normally, anyone could have done this. Pilate would not have been involved; an underling would have been delegated for this job. I was puzzled why Pilate was concerning himself with this smalltime preacher named Jesus. I also noticed something strange about Pilate. For the first time in my life, I found him to be extremely nervous. He paced back and forth, wringing his hands. I'd never seen him that way before. He always seemed to have a command of the situation. For the first time, I saw a chink in his armor. He told me to go and get dressed and to return immediately, for it would not be long until Jesus would be handed over. I remember going back to my quarters and getting ready. I mentioned to one of my cohorts why Pilate had called me. I remarked how nervous Pilate was.

1

My friend said that he understood. I asked, "Why? I mean, I don't understand. Why is Pilate so upset about this preacher? We've had preachers before, we've put them to death before, we've punished them before. Why is this one so special?" And my friend said, "For a number of reasons. First and probably foremost is the fact that Claudia, Pilate's wife, has been sneaking off, listening to this man called Jesus. She has gone not once or twice, but at least a dozen times, and each time she's come back to tell her husband about this peaceful man. And Pilate's worried. He doesn't really understand who this Jesus is, but his wife seems to be infatuated with him and his preaching. And secondly, this Jesus claims to be the Messiah, the savior who's to come and save his people. And Pilate's nervous about that, too." I smiled and said, "Well, I'm going to love this assignment. If there's anything I can't stand, it's the self-righteous type who thinks he's God's gift to the human race."

Pilate summoned me about nine that morning. The Jews were to hand Jesus over at that time and they refused to hand him over to anyone except Pilate, himself. I stood there as this Jesus was handed over. I looked at him. He was a thin but well-muscled individual and stood about six-two. What one was most drawn to about him were his eyes; a deep pool of blue. They seemed to have a calming quality. My first thought was that he probably could convince anyone of anything.

Pilate took this Jesus into his inner chambers. I was told to come with him. Pilate began to quiz him. I was puzzled at Pilate's questions. What was he trying to prove? What was he going to do with this Jesus? And then it suddenly dawned on me that Pilate was not asking the questions of the prisoner just to try to find something for which to punish him. He was looking for the peace that his wife had found in this person Jesus. Pilate was still nervous. I saw how uneasy Pilate was in Jesus' presence. Eventually he sent me away, because Jesus didn't seem very cooperative in talking with Pilate while I was present.

About a half hour later, Pilate called me back and told me to take Jesus down to the courtyard and scourge him. I was puzzled. But then, you never asked Pilate any questions, you just did as he told you. And so I took Jesus down to the courtyard and had him scourged. And one of those under me asked, since we didn't have to return him so quickly, if we might not have some fun with him. I thought that might be a good idea because I wanted to see the mettle of this man. They found a cloak which in its day might have been very beautiful. They wrapped it around him. We spat at him. But something strange happened: he didn't rebel. He just sat there. I wondered how long it would take for him to react. But he didn't. Of course, I'd seen men like that before. A little while more, I thought, and he would crack.

I brought him back to Pilate. Before this day, Pilate had always seemed to be in control of everything: a man with no emotions. But as he looked at Jesus, I saw tears begin to form in his eyes. As he took Jesus back in front of the Sanhedrin, he said, "Look!" I knew then what his hope was. Having seen Jesus beaten as he was, Pilate thought the Sanhedrin would say, "It's all right, you can let him go now." But they didn't. They kept yelling, "Crucify him! Crucify him!" And Pilate was torn. He knew this man was innocent. He knew this man to be good. But they kept shouting, "Crucify him!" And eventually they said the magic words: "If you don't put him to death, we will tell Caesar!" Pilate said, "All right."

I felt for Pilate as he stood there. I felt for him because so many times in my life, I knew the right thing to do, but let the rest of the world tell me what I had to do. Pilate knew that the right thing to do was to release Jesus, but the crowd would not let him do it. Had I been in Pilate's place, I probably would have done the same. How many times have you been placed in the same kind of situation? You know what you ought to do, but the crowd around you tells you 'no'. And instead of doing what you know is right, you let them dictate your activities.

Pilate washed his hands and walked away. But I saw his tears. He knew that by washing his hands, he did not wash himself of this ordeal, but he was afraid of what others would think. Then he turned to me and said, "Give him the cross."

3

You know that we Romans have two ways of punishing people. The first is scourging — for a man who does not deserve death but needs some kind of punishment. For more serious crimes, our method of execution is crucifixion. But in our Roman tradition, no man except this Jesus had ever received both.

At first, as I said before, I didn't understand why Pilate had asked me to have him scourged. But then I realized why: it was the hope that once they saw him scourged, they would release him. So here was Jesus already beaten and scourged and mocked, now asked to carry the cross. I share this with you only because of my utter amazement that your friend accepted the cross without a murmur. I would have figured Jesus to be very angry, and having been so severely beaten, very reluctant to accept that cross. But then, your friend Jesus amazed me all kinds of ways that day. He accepted the cross with a smile. I stood there in awe and looked into his eyes and for the very first time, I felt a sense of genuine peace. The nod of his head told me that he did not blame me for what was taking place. I cannot put into words how I felt. At one and the same time I felt guilty for what I was asking this Jesus to do and yet I felt he had this great need to grasp his cross. It was almost as if this would lead to something greater than we could imagine. I know that when I am judged by someone, my anger flares. When someone blames me for anything, I try to turn it around and blame everybody around me. And I do it angrily. This friend of yours taught me a lesson that Friday. He taught me to slow down. He taught me to strive to understand the events and the people around me. I've never been the same since that day and I feel a lot better now than ever before.

What happens when people accuse you? Do you become angry like me? Do you begin to accuse people around you for what is happening? That's the way I was until I saw Jesus in action.

I knew he wouldn't get very far with that cross, for he was so weak. But as I said before, your friend really amazed me. He fell about a hundred yards after he'd started carrying the cross. I would have stayed where I was. What sense was there in getting up to experience more pain? Why go forward, knowing that crucifixion lay ahead of you? But there he was, struggling to get up, to go on.

What I learned at that moment was that if I had a dream, if I had a goal in life, then I couldn't let anything get in the way: no pain, no hurt, no sorrow. For that dream is really worth any price.

I didn't understand it then. I do now. He had a goal, a dream, a mission and nothing would stop him from accomplishing that goal.

Before that day I had had many dreams and goals. But the difference between us was that, every time I ran into a little bit of trouble, I'd change my goal, I'd change my dream. How many times has that happened to you? You set a goal for yourself. You truly believe this is really what you want. You strive for it until you run into a stone wall and then you say, "Well, I guess that's not really what I want to do after all." You back off then and choose something else to do.

Jesus was saying his dream was worthwhile, no matter what the cost. I began to reflect on my goals and my dreams. How worthwhile were they?

Anyway, Jesus got back up and he began to struggle once again. We had just reached a bend in the street and there, at the bend, stood a beautiful and distinguished-looking lady. I must share with you that I rarely use the word 'lady'...only it was really appropriate. This was a lady. She stood out, and you knew by her bearing that she was something special. There was a hush in the crowd. Up to this point, they'd been yelling and screaming and jeering at Jesus. In fact, they became angry with him when he fell! But there was no yelling and screaming around this lady. I wondered why and I wondered who she was until one of my cohorts said, "That's his mother."

Jesus stopped. He looked at her. She looked at him. No

5

words were spoken. Yet, in their silence, much was said. I was amazed, and I was envious. So many times I'd filled the air with words. I feared silence. And yet here was this man, looking at his mother with no words spoken, yet so much happening between them. And I suddenly realized how stupid and silly so many of my conversations had been. And I envied your friend and his mother and the way they spoke with their eyes and their hearts. How many senseless and stupid words I'd used in my life just to carry on conversation.

This Jesus began to get to me and I'll tell you something: I didn't like it. I could see him becoming weaker as he went along. I felt for him. I also wanted to get this job over with. It would have been unseemly for me to have helped him. I mean, after all, I was a Roman and he was a mere Jew and one going to be put to death, at that. I scanned the crowd and saw what I needed. He was a big, powerfully-built man, looking around, trying to figure out what was going on. I thought... there's the man. I grabbed him. He was first reluctant and pulled his arm away from me. I said, "Come here!" He came. His name was Simon and he had come from the village of Cyrene. He was a farmer in town to buy some provisions and had happened to walk into the middle of this whole mess. He kept protesting that he didn't want to get involved. I reminded him of who I was and what I could do to him if he didn't do what I told him. Very reluctantly, he took the beam of the cross. As Simon began to help your friend Jesus with the burden of the cross beam, I looked at Jesus again and I could feel the peace flowing from him. Not only toward me but toward Simon, as well. With no words spoken, he was saying, 'Thank you. Thank you for the help.' If he only knew I wasn't doing it to help him, I just wanted to have this affair finished. But you know, the peaceful look of Jesus got to Simon. As Simon began to lift the beam, his reluctance was gone and he smiled back at Jesus. Simon almost looked as if he now had a sense of purpose.

I learned a valuable lesson that day. You see, before that afternoon, I had spent my whole life running away from people with problems. I didn't care. If you had a cross, that was your problem. I didn't want you looking to me for help. If you did catch me, my advice would have been that you learn to carry it yourself. The lesson I learned was twofold. I realized how much fulfillment I had lost in running away instead of helping others with their crosses. If you had told me this before that afternoon, I would have told you that you were crazy. But now I could see it just in the expression on Simon's face. The second part of the lesson is what we might call the reality factor. Just because Simon was helping Jesus with the cross didn't mean the cross was removed from Jesus. It was just easier to carry. Since that afternoon, I have not run from others with problems. I have reached out to help, but with the realization that my help might make it easier but would not eliminate the cross.

Sweat and blood now poured from the face of Jesus. A young lady from the crowd came rushing forward. She had a cloth. I later found out that her name was Veronica. She began to wipe his face. And as she did so, the crowd jeered and swore at her. But she didn't care. She just didn't care. She loved this man Jesus and what he stood for. She didn't care what anybody else thought about that. She was a lady of conviction. She lived what she believed. I only wish I had the courage of my convictions. I'm always concerned with what others think. Maybe it's because I don't think other people approve of my thoughts and my ideas and so I don't have the courage to stand up and be a person of conviction. I pray one day to be able to stand on my own two feet and have the courage of my convictions.

How about you? Do you believe in yourself? Do you have faith in what you claim to believe? Or are you always seeking approval from other people that what you're doing is all right? Or do you have the courage to stand up for what you believe and have faith in yourself because He has faith in you? I don't know if I could do what Veronica did. I pray one day I can.

It was now about midafternoon and the sun was beating down on us. Sweat was rolling off me and I could just imagine the pain that Jesus was feeling, but at this point I didn't care. I just wanted to get this whole thing over with. But even with Simon's help, Jesus, beaten and sweaty, fell again. This time I became angry at him. I wanted this whole thing over with and he

7

was delaying the whole process. I thought how often I'd done that in my life, how often I'd thought of myself rather than what the other person was feeling. I began to prod him with my stick, saying, "Come on! Let's go! Let's get this thing over with!" You see, he was getting to me and I didn't like that. As I prodded your friend to get back up, he sensed my frustration and looked at me and he smiled in a way that said he understood and he was sorry that he was causing me so much inconvenience. Here he was, in so much pain, and he was saying, "I understand. I'm sorry for causing you so much delay." As I watched him get back up, I felt so ashamed. I went back in memory and saw all the times in my life when I just wanted to do something and I didn't give a damn about anybody else or what or how they felt. I didn't care about them. And there I was, doing it again. He was innocent. He hadn't done anything wrong. He was lucky to have made it that far. I was so ashamed. How many times in your life have you done the same thing, only caring about what you wanted to do? You didn't stop to think how that might affect other people. You didn't stop to think how it might hurt them or stunt their growth. What a lesson he taught me.

The pace was much slower now. I didn't have the heart to push him to go any faster. At another corner of the street, there were some women. All of them were crying. I noticed them because they were in sharp contrast to the rest of the crowd who were watching the events unfold, some taking an active part by jeering and calling Jesus names. The women's tears seemed to be, at one and the same time, tears of sadness and tears of frustration because they were unable to do anything to stop what was happening to Jesus. He stopped and he smiled at them and told them it was going to be all right. For the first time in my life, I saw a man gain strength from another person's tears. As I reflected on it in the days afterward, I began to understand that those tears were telling your friend Jesus that what he was about was worth it. That those tears gave him the courage to go on. And I began to think of all those times in my life when others gave me the encouragement to go on, with just a smile, a pat on the back, or even a tear. Where would I be now without those people? Without their smiles or their tears? I realize now how ungrateful I've been to those who love me. How

I've taken their love for granted.

As hard as Jesus was trying, he fell again. He just didn't have the strength to go on. And I became angry again, but this time I wasn't angry at him. I was angry at all those people around who were yelling and screaming at him to get up and continue down the road. Do you know, I've heard such jeers before with other prisoners I've led to crucifixion and it never seemed to affect me. I didn't care then. I wondered why it began to bother me now. I wondered why I was upset with the crowd. Then it came to me. In the past, I'd been filled with apathy. Who cared? I didn't care. But now, for some reason, I did care. I cared what happened to this man. Maybe it was because I had the feeling that this man was innocent...not only innocent, but kind and understanding and loving. I began to think then of all the times in my life when I just hadn't cared what was happening to someone else. Apathy. Not caring. Something only a non-sensitive person would be. I thought of all those times and I felt very sick.

Jesus eventually got back up and we journeyed forward. Finally, we were on the hill called Golgotha. I knew what was to happen next. I'd been there before and I dreaded the next step. Jesus' blood had begun to dry on his clothes. And now I had to take those clothes off. I knew how painful this was going to be and how it would reopen all those wounds. I tried to do it as gently as possible as tears welled up in my eyes. He smiled and he nodded and he touched my hand and when I finally got the robe off, I wanted to say 'I'm sorry,' but I couldn't find the words. But an extraordinary thing happened. He looked into my eyes and I looked into his and we didn't need words. We spoke those words 'I'm sorry,' and 'It's all right,' without uttering them aloud. He was saying "Thank you for being gentle." We spoke without words and yet our hearts touched. What I had desired when I saw him meet his mother Mary, I now had.

The next step was even more painful than the last. I knew my cohorts were expecting him to scream and blaspheme as the nails entered his body, but somehow I knew better. In just three short hours I felt I had come to know this man called Jesus more than someone I'd known all my life. In that short time, I knew more than anything that he was a man for others. As the nails were driven in, I heard him say, "Father, forgive them, for they know not what they do." I wasn't expecting him to holler and scream but I never expected those words. And I thought about all those people in my life that I seemingly hated. All those people I sought revenge against and would not forgive. And I found myself echoing his words, "Father, I forgive them."

There were two thieves crucified with him that day. It's amazing how people react to different situations. There was the one on his left, swearing and cursing at him just as the crowd had done, saying, "If I could get close enough to you, you would feel the sting of my fist!" The thief on Jesus' right began to reprimand the one on the left, saying, "What's happening to us, we deserve. But he doesn't." And, instead of his hands being clenched, he opened them up and reached toward Jesus, though they couldn't touch. He said, "Jesus, remember me when you come into the kingdom." And Jesus turned his head and smiled and said, "Today, you'll be with me in paradise."

It was about three o'clock when he said, "It is finished," and his head went down. The normal procedure in crucifixion is that we break the legs of the one being crucified so that he eventually suffocates and dies. One of my cohorts took up a stick to break his legs. I grabbed the stick and threw it away. "Don't touch him," I said. He looked at me and said, "But it's procedure!" I said, "Don't talk to me about procedure." I took a spear and threw it into his side. I did it, not because of procedure, but because I wanted to make sure his agony was over.

I watched as they took him down naked, and I thought how much we had humiliated him. Here was this beautiful human being whom we had humiliated to the last. I thought, too, how this man came into the world naked, and was leaving it in the same way. And I thought about how concerned I am with material goods. I must have the best of everything. And yet here was a man who never had a pillow for his head and yet was filled with peace. And I thought of all those material goods that I had piled up in my life and I asked myself whether they had brought peace. The answer was a resounding 'no'. Yet in three hours, he had brought me that peace. Here was Jesus, even in death, teaching me that material things mean nothing. What counts is that you are true to yourself. Here was a man who truly was faithful to the last.

A man from Arimathea named Joseph and a few of his friends carried Jesus to a tomb. Pilate had sent word that I was to follow them and make sure he was buried. Pilate, still under the pressure of the Sanhedrin, was told that Jesus had made the bold threat that, if he were put to death, he would rise on the third day. The Sanhedrin demanded that an armed guard be put in front of the tomb so that Jesus' friends would not come and steal the body. As a result of all the pressure, Pilate ordered me to stay at the tomb and make sure Jesus' body remained in that grave. Even with as much respect as I had gained for this Jesus, I can honestly share with you that I did not expect anything to happen. Even though he had said he would raise himself up from the dead, I knew that not even God Himself could do that. So I stayed to see what would happen. And it was on that first day of the week that the ground began to tremble. My cohorts ran because they were afraid. But I stood there. And I watched the rock move. And he came forward. We embraced. And I heard myself say, "I love you."

You see, your friend became my friend that day. Your friend taught me so much in such a short period of time. He taught me that peace is to be found in caring, that we must strive to understand each other, that we must give each other the benefit of the doubt. He taught me my need to have dreams, and to be willing to do anything to achieve those dreams. But most of all, he taught me to be a believer in myself. He will forever be my friend.

PETER

My name is Simon. You probably know me better by the nickname that our mutual friend, Jesus, gave me. He called me the Rock, or Peter.

I suspect that if I were to ask you what you already know about me, you would say one of two things: either that I was the leader of the twelve, better known as the apostles, or that I was the one who three times denied the fact that I even knew Jesus. And that would be O.K.

I come before you today, almost compelled to do so, to share with you who Jesus was to me. You see, it is my firm belief that we each come to know who Jesus is, not only by our own encounters with Him, but also by the encounters of others with Him. I think it is necessary for us from time to time to share with each other who that Jesus is for us. And I think that it is in this way that each of us comes to know our mutual friend, Jesus, in a deeper way, enabling us to grow in relationship with Him even more deeply.

For you to understand who Jesus is to me, you perhaps need to understand a little about me and my background.

My parents were rather strict Jews, so it followed that my brother Andrew and I were raised very strictly as old-fashioned, conservative Jews. I was taught, from a very early age, the work ethic. Work hard at what you do and do the best at what you do and you will be wealthy; wealthy in friends and family, and you will live to a ripe old age. I was taught to be leery of certain people and nationalities. And I was taught that very special philosophy — an eye for an eye and a tooth for a tooth. I was taught, too, that the pharisees and scribes were my leaders and mentors and I should listen to what they said. That I should be a student of the Ten Commandments and obey them. If I did this, everything would be right with my world and my God. And I believed this.

My father, John, was a fisherman, in business with his friend Zebedee. Andrew and I worked with our father as did Zebedee's sons, John and James. In all honesty, we were excellent fishermen. And we made a good, comfortable living at it. That is not to say that we were rich, but our families never had to want for anything.

When I was sixteen, like most Jewish lads, I took a bride. Her name was Elizabeth. We had two daughters and a son.

If my wife were to try to describe me to you, I think she would call me a very caring and loving man — a hard worker — a man who is concerned about his fellow man but who, at the same time, is a very proud man, quick of temper, who seldom thinks before he speaks. My mother-in-law says that I am the only man she knows who can open his mouth and insert both feet at the same time.

To sum up, I see myself as a man filled with weaknesses as well as strengths. I became a better person because of my friendship with Jesus. This is not the whole story of that friendship but a few of the more important aspects of our relationship as I traveled this road of conversion with Him.

How did I come to meet Jesus? One day after fishing, I came home and my wife, Elizabeth, with a great smile on her face and an aspect of excitement about her, couldn't wait until dinner to tell me what had happened that day.

It seemed that she had been in the village that day. A young man came to the square and began to preach. Many had gathered to hear Him. The man's name was Jesus. He came from a small village called Nazareth. She told me she had never heard such a preacher. She said she was amazed at the peaceful and calming effect He had on those who were listening. She said He spoke in a soft voice, never once raising it. He spoke of peace and love. She said only a man at peace with himself could preach in such a way. She couldn't wait to hear Him again and asked if I might not go and listen the next time He was around. I grunted a 'maybe'.

The next Sabbath, He came back. Elizabeth came to me and said, as only she could, "You promised you would go if He came again." I can never understand how a "maybe" can so easily turn into a "promise". Anyway, I went.

As I sat there and listened, His preaching shook my very roots, because some of the things He spoke of were things that seemed to contradict what my parents had taught me. He talked about love, which I later found was His predominant theme. I heard Him saying to me "Forget the idea of an eye for an eye and a tooth for a tooth. Instead, love your enemies, do good to those who hurt you, turn the other cheek."

As I listened, I realized that what my wife had said was true. He never once raised His voice, was very calm and seemed very much at peace with Himself and His God. But what He had to say upset me greatly. It was difficult to sit there and listen. At the same time, I felt compelled to listen because I had never really heard anyone say the things He was saying. And what worried me was that He was making some sense.

I was an old-fashioned Jew and up to this time, I liked the fire and brimstone approach of preaching — the style of John the Baptist. The Baptist had really caught my imagination. But now, I felt that this Jesus was somehow touching my heart. I really struggled with this. In a way I was saying to myself, I really don't want to hear this. This was in opposition to what my parents taught me — so different from the way I was brought up.

Elizabeth and I went home that night and discussed what this Jesus had said. I still wasn't terribly caught up with the man. But I told her that the next time He was around, I would be willing to go and listen to Him once again.

A month or so later, Jesus returned. Both Elizabeth and I went to listen to Him. The more I listened that day, the more I got caught up with this new message of peace and love. This is not to say I had removed all my doubts. I hadn't. But then He said something that made me realize that perhaps Jesus and I were not coming from different directions after all, but from a single direction. He said, "I have not come to change the law but only to fulfill it." His statement came like a bolt of lightening. I felt He was reading my mind! As He went on, I began to read between the lines. I had the feeling that what He was saying was, "Don't be afraid of what you were taught in the past. It was good. But what I'm asking you to do now is to be open and to go beyond the past — to live in the present and plan for the future." This was echoed by my friend Paul many years later: "When I was a child, I did the things of a child, but now that I'm an adult, I have put away the things of a child and live as an adult."

And so as I listened to Jesus, I began to lose my fear of His message. What I lived in the past was all right. It was good for me at that time. But I needed to be open now, and to see new ideas that would help me grow in relationship with my God in heaven. The more I listened, the more I was impressed.

I wonder sometimes if you might not feel the same as I did — so many times caught up with what we were taught in the past, fearful of change, fearful of being open, of being free.

Maybe the message Jesus had for me long ago is the message He has for you now. Maybe He is just asking you to be open — open to the new — to be open to the present — to plan for the future — so that your relationship with the Lord might grow more fully.

It wasn't long afterward that I personally encountered Jesus. My brother Andrew and I, along with John and James, had been out fishing, this time for eight hours, with little success. My patience had run out; my temper was flaring. My brother and friends knew exactly how I felt.

As we came toward shore, I saw Jesus, with a large crowd following after Him. He approached me, smiled, and asked if He could use the boat for a while. I asked why. He said, "Well, if we could pull out just a little way, we could get the crowd seated on the shore and I could preach to them." I said, "Why not — nothing else worthwhile is happening on this boat." We rode out a little way. He began to preach. As I sat there in the boat, I realized what a compelling preacher He was. He talked about the fact that He had come to make His heavenly Father known. He talked about how loving and forgiving this Father was. He talked about our spreading this good news around about this loving Father. I could not help but think that in the past I had always pictured God as a very stern but caring Father, much like my own father who believed in the old proverb: He who spares the rod hates his son, but he who loves him takes care to chastise him.

When He had finished, the crowd applauded Him. He smiled and thanked them for listening and for being so open to His words.

He then turned to me and (almost as if to say 'I want to repay you for the use of your boat and for your precious time,') He said, "Why don't you pull out a little way and lower your nets." And to prove what my mother-in-law used to say about inserting both feet in my mouth, I said, "Jesus, I know you're a good preacher, perhaps the best I've ever heard, but I am a good fisherman — perhaps the best you'll ever meet. And I'm telling you the nets won't bring anything up! There aren't any fish to be had!" I'm afraid I even implied to Him that He should stick to preaching and leave the fishing to me.

He shook His head, smiled and said, "Please, just humor me and drop your nets." I was proud of myself because this time I didn't lose my temper. I decided to drop the nets to show Him I knew what I was talking about. Within minutes the nets were overflowing with fish! I was forced to call James and John over with their boat to help me.

I looked at that filled net—and I looked at Him—and I looked at his gentle blue eyes and the smile on His face. His expression said, "Thank you for letting me use your boat. Thanks, too, for humoring me."

I'd never met a man like that before! I was truly humbled in His presence. And I, a very proud man, did something I had never done before. I humbled myself before another man. I got down on my knees. I said, "You know, Lord, I made a fool of myself a little while ago. I told you to stick to preaching and I would stick to fishing. I'm beginning to understand, Lord, that you're not just a preacher of religion, but you are the Lord of all things."

And let me tell you something, dear friend. I had real tears in my eyes. I felt so small, kneeling before Him, and I admitted I was a sinner and didn't deserve to be in His presence.

He smiled, reached out and lifted me up. He said, "You know Simon, you and I make a good team. If you really believe what you said, would you consider coming with me and doing as I am doing—fishing not for fish but for men?"

I looked at Him with some puzzlement and didn't stop to think of what He meant, I just answered, "Yes!" I realize now that I said 'yes' at that moment because I was thinking not so much of how I could reach out to others, but more of what this man could do for me—and how much I could learn from Him.

I learned two invaluable lessons that day. The first was that the Lord wasn't just the Lord of religion or faith but rather He was the Lord of all things. I am sure that in many ways, you do what I did that day. We have a tendency to divide things up into compartments. We want to categorize things and we put the Lord over here—our family and friends there—other things over there. It is a lot like a pie—we cut it up and say this portion is the Lord's—this is mine—that's yours. But in reality, the whole pie is the Lord's. On that day I had assumed that the Lord was the Lord of a way of life while I was the Lord of the sea. What I came to learn that day was that my sea was just part of His Way. What I came to learn was that wherever I was, the Lord was there. Whatever I was about, the Lord was about. For He is the Lord of all things.

The second lesson I learned was that when we say 'yes' to the Lord, we sometimes think that we're saying "Yes, I want to reach out to others"—"Yes, I want to do what you want." But the bottom line is, that if we want to say yes to the Lord and what He wants us to do, then it is we who benefit far more than He or anyone else we touch with our lives. For it is in saying yes to the Lord that we will come to know the true meaning of life. These lessons were important on my journey down Conversion Road with the Lord.

After this incident, I went home to tell my wife the events of the day and throw some things together for my journey. I was amazed by her reaction. She was happy for me and of course there was also some pain because she knew we would be separated for a while. She also said she knew that I had been searching for something and that this opportunity might be that something. It was strange because I didn't even realize I had been searching. Isn't it marvelous that someone who loves you can sometimes know you even better than yourself?

I left the next day. For the next few weeks, John, Andrew, James and I journeyed with Jesus and picked up a few other men along the way—a tax collector named Matthew—an accountant named Judas. Each time we entered a village and Jesus preached, the rest of us would stand in awe. Even though some of what He preached we had heard before, there was always something new that we learned by the way He would present it. I was on fire but didn't really know why! He was touching my heart and maybe for the first time in my life, I was beginning to understand the meaning and purpose of life.

Weeks stretched into months. From time to time we would get back to our own village. I couldn't wait to share with my wife what I had learned. But, as I told you before, I am a man of weaknesses as well as strengths. The worst of those weaknesses (my pride) began to raise its ugly head and grow by leaps and bounds.

You see, when we began to make second rounds around the villages, people not only recognized Jesus but they began to recognize me and my brother and the others. We were treated with great esteem. They recognized us as special, and this started to feed my self-esteem. I began to return to my old ways, doing and saying rather stupid things—all because of that pride within me.

Let me give you some examples. One night Jesus and we twelve set up a camp between two villages. We had a good fire going as we all sat in a circle. I noticed that Jesus was a bit tense that night. Something was bothering Him; He was depressed. As we sat around that fire, He began to speak. It was almost as if He just had to get this off His chest and thought what better place than with His loving friends. His beautiful eyes glistened with tears as He shared with us that He would be going up to Jerusalem where He would be arrested and crucified.

That's when I opened my big mouth and said, "No way! I won't let it happen!" He looked up at me, hurt. I knew He was crushed. He had unburdened His soul to us and instead of receiving our concern and compassion and understanding, He found that we weren't even listening to His cry of anguish. He looked at me and His look said, "I don't necessarily want it to happen either, Peter, but it will happen." Instead of keeping my mouth shut, I continued to argue. Finally He stood up and said, "Get behind me, Satan." He then walked off to be alone. As I look back on it now, I'm sure He felt very desolate. He had shared with us this heavy burden so that we could help Him carry it—and here we were arguing that there was no need to carry it.

You see, the real reason I told Jesus it wasn't going to happen and I wouldn't let it happen was that although I was concerned about Him, I was even more concerned about myself, and what would happen to me. I was so locked in my own point of view that I failed to understand His. I think we all go through that in life. Instead of looking to what the Lord wants or what someone needs, our reaction is: "What is all this going to mean to me? How am I going to handle that, or what am I going to get out of that?" Sometimes our actions and reactions aren't so much of what's good for the other but more what is best for me.

I slept poorly that night—thinking about what I said and did. I went to Jesus the next morning and apologized. He looked at me and smiled and said that it was all right.

But you know—I didn't learn my lesson there. What I didn't realize at the time was that when you hurt someone and say you are sorry, the only way you can prove that sorrow is to work on the cause of the hurt. The cause of Jesus' hurt was my selfishness and pride. Instead of working on it, I think it even worsened.

Just to give you another example about that—we had been working hard one day near the Sea of Galilee. When evening came, Jesus felt the need to go off and pray for a while. He told us to get in the boat and go to the other side. He said He would join us later. We began to make our way across. It was about midnight when we saw something on the water. Most of us were filled with panic, thinking it was some sort of ghost. Then the object spoke. It was Jesus. "Don't be afraid," He said, "It is I."

I immediately shouted—"If it is really you, Lord, have me come to meet you in the water!" (There I was opening my mouth again.) He said, "Come." I climbed out of the boat and, there I was—walking on water—my eyes fixed on Jesus. Suddenly I realized what I was doing. I—Peter—was walking on water. Swelling with pride, I took my eyes off Jesus and looked back to my friends. The stupid grin on my face was saying, 'Do you see what I'm doing? It's a miracle!'

And you know what happened? I began to sink. Jesus reached out and pulled me out. "When are you going to learn, Simon?"

You see, our pride is not only expressed in our words—but also our actions. Because I had taken my eyes off Jesus and tried to do it on my own—I began to sink. And that is pride.

How often we all do that. Not walking on water, of course, although some of us think we can do that. Our pride is expressed every time we believe we can succeed completely by ourselves—with no one's help—not even the Lord's. And nine chances out of ten, what happened to me happens to all of us, we begin to sink. We sink because of our blind pride—we fail to keep our eyes on the Lord, and on our goal.

And if you think about it a minute, you'll realize that the lesson I learned that day was the lesson I should have learned on the first day I met Jesus and caught all those fish—that the Lord is the Lord of all things.

You see, my friend, what we learn is of little value until we put it into our lives and act on it. As you can see, at this point of my life I had not come to that conclusion.

Have you learned that lesson yet?

You would think that after an incident like this, I would start talking to myself and coming to grips with my pride and selfishness. I was learning but not putting into practice what I was learning. There were a few more instances before I learned my lesson. You see, one of my other weaknesses is my rather thick head.

We were making our way to Jerusalem now. In one of the villages where we stopped, Jesus began to preach. We stood in the back. The crowd was large. Jesus was preaching on judging others. He was telling them it was up to the Lord to judge. It was up to us to love. There was a young woman named Mary Magdalene present, a prostitute. She came to Jesus afterwards. As they talked, I could see by the expression in her eyes how deeply she was caught up in what Jesus had said and what an effect it had on her. He reached out and touched her, and she smiled. A very pretty young girl had approached Him—but after he had touched her, she was aglow. And she was now a beautiful lady.

She began to tag along with us—along with some other followers of Jesus. And you know for some stupid reason, I was upset with that. I was thinking: Hey, wait a minute! We twelve were supposed to be special, and here was this common prostitute, who comes into our midst and becomes equally important to Jesus. There was pride again—in my judgment of her.

Jesus sensed it and took me aside. He said, "Simon, Mary is a very beautiful person who has so much good within her. Don't judge her. Let her come to full blossom."

I knew deep down within me, He was speaking the truth. Here I was making judgment on her—and I was filled with pride and selfishness and jealousy.

I even remember Jesus preaching about that once. He asked the pharisees and scribes how it was that they could see the speck in their brothers' eyes and not see the timber in their own.

Isn't it funny how we judge others through our own prejudiced eyes rather than seeing them as who they really are? Isn't it funny, too, that we see ourselves with the same prejudiced eyes and think nothing of it?

Anyway, we finally made it to Jerusalem and the thing that Jesus had predicted came true. They arrested Him and took Him to the Sanhedrin. They arrested Him that Thursday night in the Garden called Gethsemane. We were all there, for that was our normal place to relax after supper when we were in Jerusalem. We also did a great deal of praying there. In fact, that was the main reason Jesus took us there that night. Sad to say, He was the only one who prayed that night. He had asked especially John, James, and myself to pray with Him. But because of the hour and our full stomachs, the three of us fell asleep.

As I reflect on that night, I think how sad it was—because once again Jesus came to share with us, his closest friends, all of His anxieties and fears, and all we could do was sleep.

When the soldiers came to arrest Jesus, I was embarrassed at what I had done—He had asked if I couldn't give him one hour of prayer and I hadn't.

As they took Him off, I wanted to make up for what I had done. I looked at John and he returned my look. And John said he knew some of the court people, and that we might follow and support Him as best we could.

The rest of the twelve, frightened at what had happened, had left—but John and I followed in hopes that at least in some small way we could be of service to Him.

We arrived at the courtyard of Caiphas where they had brought Him. John talked to someone at the gate and got us admitted. They had already taken Jesus inside.

It was cold that night, and fires had been lit in the courtyard. I stood near one of the fires with my hands outstretched. I merely remarked, "It's cold tonight," when one of the servants looked up. He said, "You are one of the followers, aren't you?" I said, "A follower of whom?" He said, "Of Jesus, of course! Your accent gives you away!" I began to swear. "Jesus? Who is this Jesus? I'm a stranger to these parts."

I backed away from the fire and slipped into the shadow of the outer wall. That encounter with the servant had unnerved me. Guilt and fear caused a sickening feeling in my stomach. The greatest thing that had ever happened to me was my friendship with Jesus—and I had just denied it even existed. I sank to the ground and sat in the darkness—my face in my hands. I don't know how long I was there. John came with his friend Cleo to tell me they were trying to get Jesus to speak but that He wouldn't.

Cleo said it was cold—she grabbed my hand and took me to the fire where they were cooking soup. The crowd around the fire began to talk about Jesus. Those who had heard Him preach said they'd known from the beginning He was up to no good. I just stood there and let them tear down my best friend and all that He and I stood for. Finally one of them turned to me. "Have you ever heard Him preach?" "No," I heard myself say, "up until tonight, I've never even heard of Him." I ran to the wall and was overcome with nausea.

As I crouched there and recovered, tears began to well up in my eyes. What am I doing? What have I done? At that point,

John came back to tell me there were no new developments. He went back, close to the house. Those who had seen the two of us talking came up to me. "I thought you said you never heard of Jesus. If you're friends with John, then you lied to us—John is one of His closest friends."

I began to shout, "I don't know Him! How many times do I have to say I don't know Him?" With that I ran out of the courtyard, tears streaming down my face.

What a fool I had been—I had chosen my well-being over His love. I had hurt my relationship with Him before, but now I had done the ultimate to destroy it: I denied I even knew Him.

The Sanhedrin had found Him guilty of blasphemy—of claiming He was God. They now took Him to Pilate to be condemned.

I stood in the street as they marched Him to Pilate. I had not been able to stop my tears since the courtyard confrontation. I didn't have the courage even to look up as He went by, but some impulse made me take a quick glimpse, and He looked right into my eyes. He was saying, 'Thank you for being here.' Stabbed by guilt, I wept all the harder—obviously He didn't know what I had done.

I slipped away to that upper room where we had had supper the night before. The rest—save John—were there. They all wanted to know what was happening. I told them and then went off into the corner to be alone. I kept saying to myself, "Never again—never again."

John returned late that evening. He told us all about what had happened on Calvary and that Jesus was dead. In that upper room, we prayed as we had never prayed before. We prayed humbly, that God would help us keep alive the message of Jesus, and we vowed, more humbly yet, to do our best to accomplish this.

It was on the first day of the week that He returned. I can't describe the mixed feelings I had—ashamed yet overjoyed that He was once again present to me.

I embraced Him. He whispered. "Thank you for Thursday night. Thank you for supporting me. I felt it."

I couldn't believe it—HE STILL DIDN'T KNOW WHAT I HAD DONE! I had expected Him to tell me of His disappointment in me and here He was thanking me.

I heard myself say, "No—no." Tears were flowing down my face. "I denied you three times. I denied I even knew you."

"Peter," Jesus whispered, "I know—I know—but at least you were there—you were trying your best and I thank you."

I knew what I had done—and maybe for the first time I knew what I was going to do. I was going to do everything in my power to prove worthy of this man's love. From that time on, I have tried to do just that. That is why I am telling you this. My friend John wrote at the end of his gospel that it was not the whole story—for the whole story could not be contained in one book.

This is not my whole life history with Jesus—that would take a lifetime to tell.

I have shared with you a small portion of my life and some of the things I learned from our mutual Friend. My hope is that you have learned what I learned:

1) You cannot live in the past—for it makes the present painful and the future unattainable. Instead, be free to look at the past as precious, the present as an adventure, and the future as a chance for fulfillment.

2) Know that the Lord seeks to be the Lord of your life—He seeks to grow in relationship with you—to be with you—in you. He wants you to know that He and you together can do all things.

3) Know that to say Yes to the Lord isn't so much a heroic act as it is the only sensible thing to do in life if we are interested in knowing life's meaning and coming to know true peace and fulfillment. They cannot be found in any other place.

4) Know that to be sorry is to say to yourself, "You don't want to hurt", and tackle the cause of that hurt within yourself.

Finally, there will be times when you will strive to do your very best and still fall short. Never put yourself down—pick yourself up and try again—and again—and again. Never be sorry you gave it your best shot.

JOHN

You might recognize me as John — one of the twelve — the evangelist — the epistle writer — or the one Jesus loved. It wasn't always that way, though. But then, that's part of the story of my journey down Conversion Road. I want to share with you that journey: how Jesus reached out to me, how He walked with me down that road that led to the Father.

I should begin at the beginning. I am the second son of Zebedee and Ruth. I have an older brother, James. We grew up in a neighborhood with two other men I'm sure you've heard of: Peter and Andrew. Their father, Jonah, and our father, Zebedee, were partners in a fishing business and were the best of friends. That friendship was a deep bond, more like a true brotherhood. Our families spent a great deal of time together as we grew up. Our fathers were God-fearing men who worked hard, played hard and prayed hard. And both taught their sons the work ethic — that you should always do the best that you can.

Growing up in such a family was an adventure. It was a time filled with love, and sometimes hurt. My mother always told me I was too sensitive and that I took things too seriously, and perhaps she was right. This sensitivity sometimes clouded my judgment and caused me some hurt. You see, it's a Jewish tradition that the oldest son — the firstborn — is the favored one and the one who inherits authority over all family matters. The sun rises and sets on him. James was the firstborn. I was often asked why I wasn't as good a fisherman as James was, and why I wasn't quite as smart as he was. But you know, that really didn't bother me. I can honestly say that I was not jealous of James. You see, I loved my father very much, and I know he loved me very much. But a father has to brag about a son who excels, and believe me, James excelled. Next to Peter, he was probably the best fisherman I ever knew. Besides that, he seemed to have it all together. I loved James just as much as I loved my father and I was really proud of them both. But it was hard living under James' shadow. It was almost as though I had lost my own identity.

In the beginning, when I introduced myself to you, I said that you might recognize me as one of the twelve, or the evangelist, or epistle writer, or the beloved of Jesus. And I said that wasn't always the case. Well, it wasn't when I was growing up or even when I was a young man walking with Jesus. My fame, my recognition, only came afterward. When I was growing up, someone would ask me my name, and I'd say, "My name's John," and they'd say, "Oh, yes, yes, you're Zebedee's son, aren't you?" or, "Yes, James is your older brother, isn't he?" I was always looked upon in association with somebody else. As a result, I didn't feel I had a great deal to offer to anyone. It seemed that my father or my brother James was always in the limelight. I was hurting. It seemed I had lost my own identity. I don't believe I knew why. It just hurt. You see, I tried to walk in another's shadow. I tried to live up to someone else's expectations. I was frustrated when someone else had a talent that I didn't have. What I needed to do was to find out who I was and be that who.

How about you? Have you had those same feelings?

My sensitivity came about in another way, too. Being good Jewish boys, and coming from good traditional families, we four boys, James, Andrew, Peter and I, were sent regularly to be taught by the scribes about Jewish traditions and heritage. I would sit at the feet of these scribes with the other boys and listen to them describe our God as awesome, and powerful, and what he seemingly had done to our ancestors because of their disobedience to Him, and heard all the rules and regulations that were placed on our people. They also taught us the marvelous things that this God had done for His people. I had some difficulty trying to picture this God who was so awesome and powerful and yet so kind to His people.

Being rather shy, I was afraid to voice my opinion to the scribes, and felt that I was the only one who thought that way, since no one else raised that question. I was having some difficulty with the God about whom I was being taught. But, since no one else voiced an opinion, I felt that I once again was out of tune with the world and should just keep my mouth shut and believe what I was told. I guess I was still living in others' shadows.

When I was almost fourteen, Jonah, Peter and Andrew's father, died. It was a difficult time, not only for them, but for all of us, because Jonah was one of the greatest men I'd ever met in my life. He was like a second father. Andrew and Peter, who by now were married, took over their father's share of the business and were still in partnership with my father Zebedee. It was about this time that Peter began talking about this new preacher called Jesus. Andrew had pointed Jesus out to Peter, but it was Peter's wife who had persuaded him to go and listen to Jesus. If you knew Peter at all, you knew he was a traditionalist. And if you knew Jesus at all, you knew He wasn't the most traditional person you'd ever meet. And so it was interesting to listen to Peter's accounts of this Jesus that first time. He would mumble things like, "He's a dreamer! He's a radical! He's crazy!" The more I listened, the more I wanted to meet this Jesus. This was the kind of person I'd been looking for. Well, I finally went to Peter and said to him, "I'd like to meet this Jesus." Peter just frowned and said, "No, you wouldn't." I said, "Well, the next time you go to listen to him, how about inviting me along?" He answered, "There isn't going to be a next time. I'm not going back to listen to him again!" So I left it at that.

Much to my surprise, about a month later, as Peter was working on the nets, he began to talk about the dreamer. When I asked what dreamer he was referring to, he shouted, "Jesus, who else? I heard him again." I sensed that although Peter protested that this man's message of love and turning the other cheek really wasn't for him, there was a change coming over Peter and I knew he had been touched. I could see a questioning going on inside him, the same kind of questioning I had had when I listened to the scribes and thought: Who really is this God about whom I'm being taught? I felt very close to Peter at that moment, and I knew how he felt. And I knew then that I had to meet this Jesus. I had to listen to him, and let him touch me as he had touched Peter.

How about you? How do you feel about the Lord? Are you open to Him? Are you willing to let Him come to you in any way that He chooses? Or, are you set in your ways? Do you already believe that you know all there is to know about Him? Are you open to new ways that He can come to you, and touch your life?

It was hard at first for Peter to let Jesus into his life. Peter was a stubborn man who thought he had everything worked out. And you know, as he listened to Jesus, what probably disturbed him most was that Jesus' words seemed to contradict his parents' teachings. But Jesus had told him, and tells us, "I've not come to change the law. I'm not come to change your life. What you were taught in the past was good. But now you are in need of a challenge, a challenge to grow." And Peter was open enough to realize that. And for that he deserved a lot of credit. He'd left a a little leeway, a little crack, in the careful structure of his life, just enough to let Jesus in. And just as Peter's wife, who had dragged her protesting husband off several times to hear this dreamer, had recognized the beauty of His words, so now Peter recognized that beauty and allowed himself to be touched.

Are you willing to listen? Do you think you know all the ways in which He can come? Are you willing to leave a little crack for Jesus to reach you in some new way? It was only because of Peter's openness that he in turn was able to touch me and bring Jesus to me. My chance to meet Jesus came not long after that. Peter and Andrew, along with my father, brother and me, had been out fishing all night. We hadn't caught a thing. And if you had known Peter very well, you would know how angry he could become. There he was, fuming on the shore, thinking of how he had wasted eight hours of energy. And there was Jesus with a crowd. And He walked right up to Peter — because He had seen Peter several times — and said, "Peter, can I use your boat for a little while?" I expected Peter to explode in frustration. Instead, he just looked at Jesus and smiled. And I thought: Jesus is really getting through to Peter. I know how he'd normally act. Peter said, "Sure, might as well use the boat for something. It surely hasn't worked for catching fish!" So Jesus got into the boat, and they pulled out a little way from shore. My father, James and I were still in our boat, but we could hear everything that was going on. And Jesus talked that day about love, about the love the Father has for each of us. About the fact that He had been sent to express that love. That He needed others to help Him in that mission, because He knew He couldn't do it alone. He talked about love and turning the other cheek, and not judging other people. As I listened, I could sense why Peter had been touched, because I now was touched by Him. After Jesus finished speaking to the crowd, He asked Peter to drop the nets over the side. I will tell you this request was really a test for Peter's temper. But Peter calmly did as Jesus had asked. I was really amazed. This was completely out of character for Peter. He just smiled at the Lord, pulled his boat out a little way, and dropped the nets over the side.

You know the story. He caught so many fish he couldn't even haul them in himself. He called us out to help. I knew then that I just had to meet this Jesus. When we finally got to shore with two boatloads of fish, Peter began to introduce me to Jesus. He made a point of telling Jesus how anxious I was to meet Him. He then introduced Jesus to my father and brother. This was the first time I had been introduced to someone before my father and brother. It was a cherished moment for me.

Jesus then turned to Peter and said, "Peter, do you believe in what I'm preaching? Do you believe in the mission that I am about?" And Peter replied, "Yes, Lord." Then He said, "You heard me preach today. I need you. Come, be a fisher of men." And, surprisingly, Peter jumped at it. I say 'surprisingly' because my friend was a great financier. He was always thinking about money, and where he was going financially in his life. But there didn't seem to be any question. What happened next was even more surprising. Jesus turned to Andrew and said, "Do you want to come along?" And Andrew answered, "Yes." Then Jesus, a traditionalist when it came to a father/son relationship, looked past James and me to look at our father Zebedee. That look said it all. He was asking my father's permission to take us along, also. My father just smiled, nodded, and walked away.

Then Jesus turned to us, and said, "John, James, I have a feeling you might want to come along." There was no hesitation as we both answered "Yes!" in unison. I don't know why James said it; I don't know why Peter said it; I don't know why Andrew said it. But I do know why I said it. My 'yes' was not initially uttered for a noble reason. It was because He had called me by name. It was because He said, "I want you." It was because He called me ahead of my brother. For the first time in my life, I wasn't in anyone else's shadow. Jesus was calling me! What a feeling! Yes, I believed in His message. Yes, I'd been looking for it since I'd been twelve or thirteen years old. Yes, I'd been looking for a man like this, to show me a way. But in all honesty, I probably said 'yes' because He had called me by name.

It was exciting as I journeyed with Him and Andrew and Peter and James. We added others on our way: Matthew, Judas... there were twelve of us altogether. And it was exciting watching Jesus go from town to town. His message never changed a whole lot. But every time you heard it, it touched you in a different way. The thing that struck me so much was that everything He said just seemed to flow from who He was. How sensitive He was.

I remember once, traveling with a large crowd. Jesus had turned down the road toward the home of Jairus, whose daughter was dying. A woman afflicted with hemorrhaging just reached out and touched Him. As soon as she did so, she was cured. And Jesus turned to Peter, who was always the spokesman for the twelve, and He said, "Somebody touched me. Who touched me?" And Peter, in all seriousness, said, "Lord, there are five thousand people here. It would be easier to find out who didn't touch You than to find out who did." The sensitivity was there. Jesus had felt His healing power go out from Him. When we eventually got to Jairus' house, the little girl, sadly, had died. Jesus, taking Peter, James and me with Him, immediately went to her bedside. I watched Him as He looked up to the Father in prayer and then reached down and gently touched her. With that, she awoke. And, again showing His sensitive nature, He turned to her parents and said, "Why don't you get her something to eat? She's probably very hungry."

I watched Him touch people. You know, we hear so much

about His preaching, but there were so many times when He would be just one-on-one with people. He would just reach out and touch them and turn their lives around. Mary Magdalene, the prostitute, was a perfect example. She came to Him one day. I watched how He talked with her, kindly, lovingly. I heard Him tell her how beautiful she was. Through that gentle conversation, her whole life was turned around.

It was thrilling being with Jesus and believing in His dream of the Kingdom. But as much as I believed in Him and His mission, I still had a hard time believing in myself. I was really proud of Peter. Any time a question was asked, Peter had the confidence to answer. He would always stand up for what he believed. At times, he was off base in what he had to say, but at least he had the courage of his convictions. I remember thinking 'Why can't I be like Him? Why can't I just get up and say what I feel? Why am I always afraid?' But I came to realize much later in life that Peter's ability to express himself so well was his unique gift. I finally came to know that I didn't need to envy that gift because I, too, had gifts that were uniquely mine. I didn't have to wish that I was Peter. What I needed to do was to strive to be the best me that I could be.

What about you? How many times do you catch yourself envying someone else's talents or situation? How often have you done so without realizing how graced and talented you yourself are? You don't need to be someone else. You just need to be you, the best you that you can be.

As I said, it was exciting to be with Him from day to day and especially so when we returned to our home town. How thrilled we were to see our families! And as soon as we got there, there were Peter's wife and my mother, fixing this marvelous big dinner to celebrate our coming home. A little embarrassing moment, though, took place right after dinner. I saw my mother take Jesus aside, and I overheard her conversation with Him. She murmured, "Lord, when you come into your Kingdom, it sure would be nice if James sat on your right and John on your left." I was appalled! But, you know, I had mixed feelings about her request and listened intently for His response. You see, I didn't know exactly what Jesus thought of me. His response might give me a clue. He looked at my mother. I think He knew I was listening. And He said, "The right and left place are not for Me to give. But can they drink from the cup that I have to drink?" I knew what that cup was. Jesus had been telling us He was going up to Jerusalem, and that there He was going to die. I didn't know whether I had the courage to drink from that same cup, but I knew I believed in Him and hoped that that belief would give me the courage I might need to do so.

It was remarkable how often Jesus told us that He was going to die. And I'm not bragging about this, but I really felt I was the only one who believed Him. All the rest kept saying, "No, it's not going to happen." That had to be wishful thinking on their part. But down deep inside, I knew it would happen. And I felt for Him because I believed in Him and His dream so much.

After that day, I still didn't know exactly where I stood, but I knew that Jesus kept looking at me and trying to draw me into Himself. He was trying to tell me that He believed in me. I didn't realize that until later on.

Eventually we reached Jerusalem. It was a beautiful day. There were all those people with palms waving and shouting "Hosanna to the son of David!" I was proud to be a follower of Jesus. This man truly was special. I thanked God that people were finally beginning to realize how special He was. Doubts even came over me now that He was going to die. With all this love being poured out for Him, how could anyone want to put Him to death? We waited through that week and I saw Jesus become angry as He threw the money-changers out of the temple. I saw Him stand up for what He believed, but with stronger words than He had ever used before. I was tempted to speak to Him, to tell Him to slow down, take it easy, that there were those just looking for the right opportunity. But I didn't. And I don't think, if I had done so, it would have made any difference. He just would have said, "I have to be me."

Thursday night came. It was the last time we were all together. He motioned for me to come and sit beside Him. He wanted me to know that although He couldn't give me the left or right side in the Kingdom, He could give me a seat next to Him at this Passover supper. And what I sensed Him saying by that motion was, 'Why don't you believe in yourself, because I believe in you.'

What a beautiful night it was. He kept saying, "How happy I am to be here. How excited I am about celebrating this day with you." Then He took some bread and broke it and said, "Take this and eat, this is My body." And suddenly I understood what he had meant on those other occasions when He said He would give us His body to eat and His blood to drink. And I took the bread and ate it. I don't know how the rest of them felt, but a change came over me. I felt a calm...at peace. I felt that in all this time in which Jesus had been reaching out for me to draw me into Himself, that I was now drawn into Him. He was part of me and I was part of Him. After we had shared the cup, He got down on His knees, preparing to wash our feet. Peter said, "You're not going to wash my feet!" But Jesus had a way with Peter. He always seemed to get what He wanted from him. He said, "Peter, if I don't wash your feet, you will have no part of Me." "Well, then, wash all of me," Peter said.

So He washed Peter's feet. And you know, as I watched Him go around doing the same for the others, I thought how humiliated I was going to be when he finally got to me. He came and washed my feet, and as He did, He looked up at me, and He smiled, and He nodded. Here was I, the youngest of the twelve, and there He was, the Son of God, washing my feet. And you know something, I was not humiliated. I felt more than ever His acceptance and His love.

Shortly afterward, we went to the garden where we had often rested while in Jerusalem. And again He took Peter, James and me along with Him. He asked if we could pray with Him. And we said we would be honored to. He went ahead a little way and began to pray. When he turned around and looked back, He found us asleep. I was ashamed when He said, "Can't you stay awake and pray with Me?" He went back to pray again, and He came back, and again we were sound asleep. It was then that the guards came to arrest Him. Embarrassed and ashamed, I felt I had let Him down. He really needed me to pray with Him, and I hadn't. I learned a great lesson. I'm a person who always says, "I'm so sensitive to other people's needs. And I can't understand why others aren't as sensitive." Well, I was ashamed for all the times I had accused someone else of insensitivity. Here I was, in one of His greatest hours of need, and He said, "Can't you pray with Me?" And by my actions I said 'No.' I felt His hurt. I felt His pain. I felt His disappointment and my own lack of concern and love. After they took Him away, I could see Peter likewise was ashamed. And he turned to me and asked, "What can we do now?" The others had run, out of fear. I said, "Well, I know someone at court. Maybe we could just follow, at a safe distance." Of course, a safe distance. Eavesdropping in the courtyard, I heard their accusations. How much they wanted Him to die! As I listened, I thought about all Jesus had done this past week. I recalled His casting the money changers out the the temple and His harsh words to the Pharisees and scribes. I had wanted to tell Him then to go easy. Recalling these events, I expected Him to fight back against His accusers. But He remained silent. And I realized that just as it took a certain amount of courage to do what He had done earlier in the week, this silence took another kind of courage. It takes a special kind of courage not to do something just to prove who you are. Jesus could have proved who He was. But He didn't do that. And that taught me a lesson. Anyone who needs to prove to others who he is doesn't really know who he is himself. I don't need to prove to you who I am; you have to learn to accept me for who I am. You don't need to prove to me who you are; I just have to come to accept you for who you are. And you see, that was a lesson I needed to learn a long time ago, when I was growing up. I didn't have to walk in the shadow of my father or my brother. I was special in my own regard. And I didn't have to prove anything to anybody. Jesus taught me that.

They finally took Him to Pilate and I knew the die was cast. He was going to die, as He had said. I don't know what happened to Peter; he somehow got away in the crowd. And I was about ready to run, myself. Until I met Mary. She looked at me, and I looked back at her, and no words would come. There were tears in her eyes and the look on her face told me that she understood. She turned then and looked at her Son, standing before Pilate, and then looked back at me. Her look was a plea: 'Walk with me — walk with Him.' Oh, I didn't want to walk with them. I wanted to return to the upper room. To be in a safe place. But I sensed her need for me to walk with her, her need for support. And so I walked. And we followed Him as He made His way to Golgotha. We watched Him as they drove in the nails. We watched as they put Him up to hang. And as He looked down at Mary and me and the other friends who had gathered, He smiled and said, "Mary, behold thy son. Son, behold thy mother." He was entrusting to me the most precious person in His life; His mother. I needed her, and so He was entrusting me into her hands, too. As she had been a source of strength for Him, she would now be a source of strength for me. He was saying in the same breath, 'I believe in you. Believe in yourself.'

I learned a couple of lessons in those few hours I walked with Mary, and witnessed the crucifixion. The first thing I learned was that we're all afraid. We're all afraid to stand up and do what we need to do. Most of the time, that fear comes from being caught up in ourselves. We begin to worry about what will happen to us. We fear that we might get hurt. We fear that we might look foolish. We fear that we might be wrong and thus be embarrassed.

I probably would not have been at the foot of that cross had Mary not asked me to walk with her. And for a moment in my life I looked at her, and just didn't have the courage to go with her. But because I saw she needed me to go, I went. That's a lesson we all need to learn. It's difficult, it's hard to do what we're called to do, but when we tie ourselves up into other people's lives and see that their need is greater than our own fear, we'll do it.

And the second thing that struck me at the foot of that cross was that I finally had come to believe in myself. I looked around, and saw that none of the other eleven were there. And I'm not bragging about that, because they had to be where they were. But for once I wasn't a follower. I stood out. I did what had to be done. How many times we do what we're called to do only if we're able to follow somebody else. Sometimes the Lord calls us, not to follow, but to stand out and to lead. I needed to walk down that road with Jesus. It was my Conversion Road. It led me to the Father. It not only taught me that I need to believe in myself, and that believing in myself, I can help that dream come to pass, but that I didn't need to walk in anyone else's shadow to do it. It taught me that the Lord called me by name, just as He calls you by name. He doesn't want you to walk in someone else's shadow, but to be yourself. He wants you to recognize your own specialness and uniqueness. He calls you to believe in yourself and to know that you are loved. He asks you to drink His cup. He will not guarantee you a right or a left seat, but as long as you're there when the kingdom comes to pass, what does it matter? I already had believed in Him. I needed to come to believe in myself. Maybe you need to come to believe in yourself, to come to believe in Him, to come to believe in His dream, to hear Him call you by name, to hear Him call you to discipleship. For Him to say, "As you believe in Me, I believe in you. Help Me bring My Kingdom to pass."

TOBIAS

You'll not find my name in the Scriptures, although I am present in one of the stories they tell of Jesus. And there they call me the rich young man. My name is Tobias and my story is quite different from the others you've read about in the Scriptures who also journeyed down Conversion Road. People like Peter and James and John and Andrew were looking for something in their lives—or at least recognized that Jesus had something special to offer them. I, on the other hand, thought I had my life well in order. They spent three years with Him. My encounter, on the other hand, lasted but a few minutes.

A little bit of background about myself might be in order before we begin. My family is wealthy. My father owns a great many farms throughout the whole of Israel and his income derives from leasing these farms. My responsibility was as rent collector for him. I also was wealthy and had everything pretty much in hand. Since my family was very religious, a very important part of my makeup was to live out the rules and regulations of my faith, to celebrate the various feasts and to offer days of atonement for my sinfulness. In other words I was very dedicated to the ritual and law of my people and was a so-called man of faith. Unfortunately it took me many years to discover that what I had called faith wasn't faith at all. In my mistaken notion of faith, I had made ritual and law my God. And what made matters worse was that I didn't even look beyond the ritualistic signs and laws to see their full meaning. As a result my so-called faith at times was merely external motions I went through or at times a faith in an institution that in a sense I was not really part of—my so-called faith was in an "it" or a "they". Because I could not or would not look beyond the ritualistic signs and law, and because I made these and the institution my "god", I failed to see a beautiful and loving God and come to know that I must invest myself in a loving relationship with this God if I were to claim I was a man of Faith.

I realize that I am far ahead of my story but I have shared

this with you for a two-fold reason. The first reason I have shared this with you is that you might now understand my reactions to my encounters with Jesus and the others who tried to bring me to Him. I would have wished that I had had these insights before these encounters.

The second reason I have shared this with you is so that you might reflect on how you and your friends see your own faith. As I look around the present world, I see that things have not changed much. In what Paul would call the Body of Christ and what you might refer to as "the Church", I see many of the same conflicts as I had. I have seen and heard those of this age refer to "the church" as an "it" or a "they". I have seen and heard people of this age either make ritual or law the center of their lives or dismiss them as being unimportant when they did not fit into their own life style. In either case there was a failure to look beyond the ritual and law to see a loving God reaching out to them in love. There was a failure to recognize that "the Church" or as Paul would say "the Body of Christ" was not an "it" or "they" but an "us". To call ourselves persons of faith, I have come to realize, we must be able to look beyond ritual and law and must come to recognize that we are the church.

Now that you know a little bit of who I am, it is time to get on with my story and journey down Conversion Road. I had always wanted to meet a prophet. I'd heard about this man called Jesus and knew He was in the vicinity. I came upon Him one day and listened to Him preach. He was different from other preachers I'd come across. Instead of fire and brimstone, He preached love and turning the other cheek. When He had finished preaching, many went up to Him individually. They seemed all to be searching—searching for information about our God, searching for cures and favors, searching for the meaning of life (theirs in particular). I felt I had no need for such questioning or searching. After all, I knew who our God was, I had learned that from the best of rabbis when I was growing up. As for favors, what could this prophet do for me that I could not do for myself. And as for the meaning of life, I guess I thought I had already figured that out and was well on my way to that kingdom of which he preached. And yet as I stood on the side watching these individuals go to Him in their search, seeking answers to their questions, walking away with expressions of peace on their faces, I felt disturbingly jealous. I would have guessed that my feeling would have been that of pity and not of jealousy. I already had what these poor people were going to Jesus for—or at least I thought I did. What I came to learn about myself from this incident was that I was filled with my own self importance—my own self righteousness—my own brand of pride—my own stubbornness. It is unfortunate that it took me years to come to these conclusions.

When the seemingly long line of individuals had come to an end, there He stood and there I stood. I so much wanted to go to Him, but, for what, I thought. I didn't need what those poor souls had gone to Him for. But then, I thought maybe He needed to hear from someone who didn't need anything from Him. Maybe He needed to hear from someone who had everything well in hand. I would go to Him now to show Him there was at least someone who had already figured everything out and He would give me the affirmation that I was going in the right direction.

And so, I knelt before Him and said, "Lord, what do I need to do in order to have the Kingdom?" He looked at me with an expression of love and replied, "My friend, the first thing you need to do is to obey the Commandments." I thought, 'Here's my reaffirmation. That's exactly what I expected Him to say.' So I smiled and replied, "I've been doing that all my life." He looked at me, again with love, and said, "I know you have. But if you really want the Kingdom, then you have to take the next step, too."

Boldly, I responded, "Name it, and I'll do it." I expected Him to say "Observe with utmost care the rituals of our Faith." But He said instead, "Take your riches, go and give them to the poor and come, follow Me." The smile remained on His face, but my smile disappeared. I could no longer look at Him, and lowered my head. What He'd just asked me to do was too much, expecting me to give up everything just to follow Him! And for what? He spoke as if He had all the answers.

Suppose I did just what He said and then discovered He wasn't the answer? I'd be left with nothing. No, I wasn't willing to take that big a risk. He hadn't pressed the issue, or scolded. He didn't ask where my trust was. He simply became silent. And so I took the opportunity to back away quietly and leave.

That was the only time I ever met Him. But in the weeks that followed, the feeling persisted that maybe I should have given Him that chance. Maybe I should have done what He asked. And the more I thought about it, the more I wondered: Am I crazy? Why would I want to do it? I like me the way I am. I need what I have. I can't give it all away to the poor! The more I thought about my encounter with Jesus and pondered the call to follow Him, the more I felt guilty for not accepting the challenge and the call. And if you are anything like me, you hate feeling guilty about anything!

It seems to me that when one feels guilty about something, he has one of two options to rid himself of that feeling. The first and obvious option is to do what it is that we have failed to do—in my case to surrender my goods and follow Jesus. The second option, the option that many of us take when we feel the cost is too high to do what our conscience says we should do, is to shift the blame from ourselves to someone else. In reference to the call I received from Jesus, I chose the second option. I felt flattered that He had called me but I felt the price was too high to comply with the call. And not liking the feeling of guilt, I shifted the blame to Him. I began to blame Him for calling me. I began to say to myself, 'How dare He think I didn't have everything in hand. Does He know all the good that I do?' And I began to make a mental list of all my good deeds—of all the caring and loving I had for others. I almost went so far as to curse Him as I pictured Him saying 'You're not doing all that you could do. I need you to do more.' And so, rather than accepting the blame and the feeling of guilt for not answering the call, it was easier to blame Him for calling me. It seemed easier to place that responsibility on His shoulders and say 'I already am a good person. I don't need to do more. You are challenging my goodness. And I can show you a list of my good deeds.'

I went about my work, looking in on my father's tenants and collecting rents. This afforded me many hours in which to think about the preacher and His impossible ideas.

It was the beginning of the Passover Week when I arrived home in Jerusalem. In the marketplace one day, I ran into my old friend, Zacheus. We'd known each other for some years, his father being one of my father's tenants. We had many a deep and soul-searching discussion, so I was aware of his feelings toward our religion, how he sometimes found it meaningless, and felt that there had to be more to faith than what he saw. I knew he still believed in a God, but couldn't believe that that God was the God of Israel. And so, for a while he had turned his back on that God of Israel and had become a tax collector. On occasion I would run into him and ask him how things were going and he would say, "All is going well for me." And so I was very much surprised when I met him in Jerusalem this time and he told me he no longer was a tax collector. I asked him why. He said, "Because I met this man and He's turned my life around." I asked, "Who is this man! I'd like to meet Him, too." Zacheus answered, "His name is Jesus."

I looked at him and exclaimed, "You are fooling me!" Zacheus said, "No, have you met Him?" I said, "Yes, and I don't want to hear any more about Him!" When Zacheus asked why, I told him my story. My friend said, "He's in town now. Come, give Him another chance. Talk to Him." And he began to tell me of all the marvelous things that had happened to him since he had given up his tax collecting and followed Jesus. I became angry with Zacheus, but angrier yet with this man Jesus. Would he not leave me alone? I'd just about forgotten what had transpired between us. And now I was reminded again of that call that had haunted me for months. I walked away from Zacheus that day and never saw him again.

Now I wondered how to resolve this nagging challenge. I had tried blaming Jesus for not seeing that I had, indeed, lived up to the Commandments. That I had already done what He had called me to do. That I didn't need to give up everything in order to achieve this Kingdom He preached.

So what was I going to do now? He had called me a second time. Not directly this time, but through Zacheus. Just when I thought I'd gotten over it, here was the turmoil again.

Needless to say, I found my excuse. This time, instead of blaming Jesus for not accepting me for the who I was, I came up with another excuse: I hate anybody who tries to force anything down my throat. And there was Zacheus, trying to do exactly that. I don't need anybody telling me what I should do. I'll make that choice myself. Zacheus was trying to push something on me that I didn't want. That made twice that this had happened.

I found excuses not to respond, but they didn't come as easily as before. Every time I turned around, I was reminded of that call, most especially that week, because that was the week that Jesus was brought before the Sanhedrin. That was the week that the crowd cried out, "Crucify Him!" That was the week He had been crucified and others claimed that He had risen from the dead. And so I had to deal with that. It was hard, but I still was not about to give up everything. I was still trying to convince myself that I was doing just fine, that I had gone far enough, that I didn't need this Jesus in my life. And I hadn't needed Zacheus reminding me of this Jesus. But the turmoil remained and I was not myself.

The smallest things began to agitate me. I had always been even-tempered and could brush things off easily. My mother and father both recognized the turmoil, although they weren't sure what it was that bothered me. Finally, my father suggested that perhaps I needed a change. And he gave me a large sum of money—a part of my inheritance—and urged me to get away for a while.

As I read the Scriptures after the fact, I likened myself to the Prodigal Son. I went off to Rome. I lived, I ate, I drank. All the things that had been precious to me—our Jewish traditions, the feasts, the Commandments handed down to the chosen people—seemingly meant nothing to me. I did as I felt like doing. I caroused, I sinned, and in the process I lost everything that my father had given to me. It was then that I realized I somehow had to get back home.

I was confused. I knew I needed to be with my family again but, at the same time, I felt embarrassed and reluctant to face them. And so, though I journeyed toward home, I took my time getting there. I found odd jobs along the way, enough for food and lodging. I was going home, but slowly.

It was on that journey home that I realized I had given up all the things that I believed in: my faith—my faith in myself, my faith in my God, my faith in my people—and I knew it was time that I got back to my relationship with God. And so in each city, I would search out the synagogue on the Sabbath and would go and listen to the Scriptures and to the words of wisdom that the scribes would share.

It was on one of those occasions, in Corinth, that I walked into the synagogue and there was a man named Paul who was preaching and I could not believe it. I thought I'd put Jesus behind me and here was this man speaking about this Jesus again! Telling me how He had come to bring the good news of the Father's love. Telling me about the Spirit that He had sent amongst His people. Telling me that he had called all of us to be born again. Calling us all to relationship with the Father in heaven. I didn't know whether to be angry or grateful. This was my third call. How lucky I was! After the service was over, I approached Paul and shared my story of how I had twice been called and how I felt this to be the third.

Paul looked at me and said, "Why don't you respond?" My reaction was twofold. I told him that, first of all, Jesus had asked me to give up my riches. But they'd already been taken away from me; I'd been stripped. I had nothing now to offer. But second, and more important, I said, my pride holds me back. It was too difficult to admit that I'd gone off in the wrong direction, down the wrong path, and that I'd sinned all along the way.

God couldn't have given me a better person with whom to share this than Paul. He merely looked at me and began to smile! I reacted with anger. "Are you ridiculing me?" Paul's response was, "No, my friend, but don't talk to me about your pride. Don't talk to me about the wrong path as if you were the only person to have gone down the wrong road. I've been there too!" With that, he began to tell me about his trip down Conversion Road. How he had gone off in the name of religion and how he had persecuted Christians. How he had put them to death. How self-righteous he had been in assuming that this Jesus would destroy his people. And how he'd had to make a complete reversal when Jesus called him to be a channel of His peace and love. He told me of the times after that conversion. How difficult it was to face a Christian assembly, not knowing in their hearts whether they should believe him or not, wondering if it were a trick, wondering how he could have just turned around so completely and entirely. I began to understand. The irony was that what Jesus had asked me to give up, I had lost anyway. And the loss hadn't really made that much difference in my life. How stupid I had been not to have accepted His call the first time around.

As I reflect on this story, I reflect on the fact that just as Samuel in the Scriptures had been called many times, not knowing exactly who it was who was calling, but finally accepting that call, accepting the will of the Lord, so the Lord never gave up on me. He continued to call me. The first call came from Him directly. But, you see, when I encountered Him in that first call, I already believed I was OK. I didn't need to give up something that I treasured—my riches. But He didn't give up on me, because He knew that at my very core I had something to offer. But we all look for excuses not to accept calls. We never place the blame on ourselves. We try to reverse that process and blame the person who has called.

And so, I took that first call and turned it around, blaming Jesus, under the assumption that He did not accept me as I was. That I already was good. I didn't need to grow and to change. And I did the same when I encountered Zacheus, except that this time I knew I couldn't use the same excuse. So I began to blame him because he was trying to force something on me. And all of these rejections of the call were because of my pride, my unwillingness to risk, because of my failure to trust.

When all was said and done, and when I had been stripped of everything, including my pride, I realized how much easier it would have been if I had just accepted the call the first time.

Thankfully, God is God and He doesn't give up. Thankfully, he used a friend like Zacheus and a man like Paul. For God was not about to give up on me. He needed me and I needed Him.

In many ways you might not think you relate to my story. You might say, "It doesn't pertain to me." But I ask you to stop and think. Could it be that my story does pertain to you and that you just don't realize it? Has your attitude been "I'm already good enough, I don't really need any more"? Maybe when you're called and you feel your conscience being pricked a bit, you've reversed the situation and begun to blame the person who's called you, rather than accepting and looking at it as it really is, at the fact that you just don't want to respond to that call or feel the cost of accepting that call is too high. Maybe we've excused ourselves by saying that we don't like things forced on us, or that we're good enough as we are. But what Jesus had asked me to do was not for His sake; it was for mine. When He asked me to give up my riches He was telling me that that was the one thing standing in the way of my fully accepting the Father's love.

Maybe there are obstacles in your life that you hold on to as much as I held on to my wealth. Maybe He's asking you to take a look at what those obstacles might be in your life. It might be your pride. It might be your selfishness. It might be jealousy. It could be almost anything. But, as you come before Him, and you ask what you need to obtain the Kingdom, be open to what He says because He's not saying it for His sake, but for yours.

I thank God He didn't give up on me. I know for a fact that he will not give up on you. He will continue to call you, continue to challenge you, reminding you that you've not grown enough. That His Kingdom can be yours only when you're willing to let go and to trust and to remember always that His call, His will, is for your happiness. I learned it the hard way. May you learn it more easily.

JUDAS

My name is Judas. Yes, I am the same Judas who handed Jesus over for thirty pieces of silver. You, no doubt, are wondering why my story would be contained in a book with Peter and John called *Conversion Road.* If you are wondering, then you must also be assuming that I did not love the Lord as they did and no longer considered Him to be friend. In both cases you would assume wrongly. Did I fail Him in regard to the love and friendship He offered to me? The answer to that question would have to be a qualified yes. At that time I thought I had acted in direct response to His love and friendship and, you see, I still call Him friend. For you to understand how I could equate my actions with love and friendship, you will need to know about my journey down Conversion Road.

I was an only son of a tenant farmer and his wife. Although as a family we barely made ends meet, I must honestly say I was never deprived of the fundamental things of life. And if I had had the choice of any two people on the face of this earth to be my parents, I could not have chosen a more loving and caring set than I was privileged to have been given. But I, like so many young people growing up, probably failed to recognize how blest I was to have such parents.

My father was an intelligent man and yet never seemed to get ahead. I inherited his intelligence. It was frustrating growing up, watching others getting ahead, knowing that I was far more intelligent than many of them. I never ever considered this a matter of pride, but of reality. At the time, I never thought that I was jealous of them. I began to realize that there was something more than just intelligence here. As I observed their successes more closely, I found two reasons for it. The first was that some of them came from a wealthier background and were surrounded by a different circle of friends. I knew, at least in the beginning, that this was not an option for me. The second reason was that the others looked for opportunities to advance themselves. Many times, they seemed to be in the right place at the right time. I say 'seemed' to be, because in reality they had been looking for that right place and right time. Now, this was an option for me. I began to spend all my waking hours looking for that right place and time. I took every opportunity to meet with people, one-on-one or in groups. I strove to ingratiate myself to them. I made sure they all knew my name, so that if my name were brought up in conversation, they would all have something nice to say about me. By doing this, I thought, I was creating my own opportunities!

As I look back on it now, I realize how foolish I was. In the beginning I said that I was privileged to have had such special people as my parents and that I was never deprived of any fundamental needs. I shared with you how intelligent my father was and that I had inherited his intelligence. What I did not tell you and did not know at the time, was that I failed to inherit his common sense. You see, as intelligent as my father was, he was also wise. So many times we confuse the two and think they are the same. They are not. My father, in his wisdom, embraced the true values in life. These values, these riches, were to be found in a loving and endearing relationship with his God, his family and his friends. When he spoke of values, he meant only the endearing relationships he had. He never would have equated values with the material things he had or the positions that he held. He never would have compromised who he was in order to obtain some thing or some advantage. He knew that the only thing of value that he could offer to others was the who he was. If he sacrificed that, he felt he would have nothing of value to offer. I'm sure he felt frustrated, at times, at his inability to give his family more in the material realm. But I am also sure he felt he gave to his family the greatest gift of all: himself. I only wish now that I hadn't spent all my energies looking for advancement, but rather had sought those real values which endowed my father with his peaceful manner.

How about you? Do you recognize the true blessings that you have? Do you sometimes confuse intelligence with wisdom? Do you look for "things" in life to give you happiness and fulfillment? Do you see friendship as something to be cherished, or a means to an end? Do you see the giving of yourself and the who you are as the most cherished gift you can give? Or do you see the compromising of yourself to obtain the prestige and honor of the world as the "intelligent" thing to do? When we consider these questions, we all know the correct responses — but do we live by them?

A thought occurred to me as I was reflecting on my father. If I were ever to have said that I wanted my children to have all the things I had never had as I was growing up, my father would have been terribly hurt. He would have been hurt because he would have thought that he had given to me all that he had: himself. How would your parents feel if you made such a statement?

Perhaps that is part of the reason I was later drawn to Jesus. As I think about it, what I recognized as intelligence and wisdom in Jesus were the same qualities that were present in my father. Due to my youth, I had failed to recognize them as I was growing up. But this is somewhat ahead of my story.

As I stated previously, I made every attempt to be known by all peoples — from shopkeepers to every organized group I could find. I was trying to create my own opportunities. It was in this context that I came to know a group known as the Zealots. I was never a member of the Zealots, but more like an outsider looking in. They were a nationalistic group of men who felt we Jews were an oppressed people. This oppression was due to the fact that we were prisoners in our own land. We had been subjugated by the infidel Romans. If we ever were to be a great people again we must throw off the chains of slavery by removing these Romans from our midst. Because of my youth, my naiveté, my lack of wisdom, and last but not least my social standing, I was very much drawn to their way of thinking. It gave me an out. After all, it wasn't my fault I was what I was. I was being oppressed by the Romans. The only part of this movement with which I was not too comfortable was their call for a violent overthrow of the government. I wasn't sure why this made me so uncomfortable — was it that I was afraid of violence, or did I think that this might be accomplished in some more peaceful manner?

It was shortly after I had been exposed to the thinking of these Zealots, that I heard about a new preacher named Jesus. At the urging of my father who had heard him, I went to find this Jesus. I had heard from one of the shopkeepers that he was in a small village just north of our own. When I finally arrived, He was already preaching in the village square. He was speaking of a kingdom, saying that it was already at hand. He spoke of peace and the love His Father has for us. He told us He was here to make His Father known and to begin that kingdom. It seemed to me that He spoke about many of the things that the Zealots had spoken of. The big difference was that Jesus' kingdom could come about without violence.

If you notice, I have used the words "it seemed". I would learn much later that there was a tremendous difference between Jesus' way of life and that of the Zealots. But on that afternoon, as I listened to Jesus, I heard what I wanted to hear. Perhaps this was because I agreed and related so much to the philosophy of the Zealots. Perhaps I listened and heard what I wanted to hear because Jesus mentioned the kingdom and peace in the same breath and I had such a hard time with the Zealots' idea of a violent overthrow of the government.

How often has that happened to you? How often have you heard what you wanted to hear and not what was really being said? Sometimes we are so desperate to be affirmed in what we believe, that we fail to hear what is really said. Sometimes we are so desperate to hear everything is all right that we fail to hear that we need to look again.

Anyway, as I listened to Jesus that day I felt that all my searching for the right opportunities had paid off. Here I was being offered the chance of a lifetime: to be in on the establishing of a new kingdom. I knew what I had to do next. I had to repeat the same ritual I had gone through before with the individuals and groups in my own village. I had to make myself known to this Jesus, and to ingratiate myself to him in such a way that He not only would catch my name but would also invite me to go along with his entourage.

I approached Him and began by telling Him who I was and where I came from. I told Him how excited I was to hear of this new kingdom and that it would be based upon an era of peace.

When I had finished my little speech, Jesus looked at me with an ever-so-slight smile. I must share with you that it wasn't the reaction I expected. The smile that He gave was not the smile of a man who thought He had just been affirmed in His beliefs. This smile was reminiscent of the smile my father would give to me when he had caught his young son doing something devious and trying to talk his way out of it. Jesus saw through me. This man was not only intelligent but He was also wise.

As I look back at that moment, I am surprised that I wasn't offended at such a look. Isn't it strange how offended we feel when we've been caught red-handed doing something devious or foolish?

Needless to say He didn't invite me along and I doubted, at least at that moment, that He even remembered my name. But the smile, the failure to invite me or know my name didn't stop me from trailing along. I don't know the precise reason why I followed Him. Maybe it was because I still saw this as a great opportunity. Maybe it was just that I was drawn to Him and found myself liking Him. As I stated before, I think I liked Him because He reminded me of my father.

Wherever He went it seemed His reputation preceded Him. No matter what village He would enter with His entourage, people would welcome Him as an old friend even though He had never been there before. In fact the crowds were getting bigger as time went on. And He was beginning to be noticed because everywhere we went some of the Pharisees and Scribes would appear as if out of nowhere. In the beginning, they just stood around and listened.

Jesus' message didn't change that much. His predominant theme was the new kingdom and how this kingdom must be based on love. It was evident that He was sincere in what He said because His actions were in complete conformity with His message. I was there when he raised Jairus' daughter. I was there when he cured the ten lepers and gave sight to Bartimaeus. I was there when, one day as we rested from a long journey, the people found us and sent their little children to touch Him. In fact I was one of those who were pulling those little ones off Him when He scolded us for it. You see He loved children crawling all over Him. He loved telling them stories by the hour. He once told us that we had to become like little children if we wanted to possess the kingdom.

I was becoming enthralled with this man. I no longer looked upon this just as a golden opportunity—I couldn't wait for the next phase of the kingdom to take place. And I was willing to do anything for Jesus. Part of my talent was that I was a great organizer. Getting from place to place with such a large entourage was no easy task. Preparing the crowds before Jesus spoke got more and more difficult. Without being asked, I began to use my organizational skills, doing the little things that made life easier.

Jesus began to notice what I was doing. He also noticed I wasn't doing it to get His attention or approval. He saw a change coming over me. And the smile He now gave me wasn't a smile that said 'I can see through you,' but rather 'I approve of your actions.' He now knew me by name (or at least I now knew He knew me by name). I knew I had been fully accepted when He put me in charge of the common purse.

There were two things I began to notice. The first was that although our entourage was growing bigger, Jesus was spending more and more time with a small group of us who came to be known as The Twelve. I felt proud to be included in this group. It was almost as if He were spending this time getting us ready to assume some special place in the next phase of the kingdom. Not only was this a golden opportunity for me but it was a time of fulfillment. I couldn't have been happier with where this was going.

The second thing I noticed and was not pleased about was that those Pharisees and Scribes who seemed to be appearing out of nowhere, were no longer sitting back and listening. They were now becoming quite vocal. It seemed at every turn they were trying to trap Jesus in His actions or His words. When He would cure on the Sabbath, He was condemned for working on the Lord's day. When He would be out for dinner, they asked why He was eating with tax collectors and sinners. This last objection always puzzled me. It seemed ironic to me that the very dinners they were objecting to, they themselves were partaking in. And if it weren't bad enough that they objected to His actions, they also objected to His teaching. They continually tried to trap Him with his own words. Once they asked Him about the greatest of the commandments. Jesus answered with the commandment of love for God, neighbor and self. They could find no fault with such an answer but thought they could catch Him by asking "and who is my neighbor?". It was then that

Jesus put them in their place — and for that matter, all of us. He told the beautiful parable of the Good Samaritan. He told of the man beaten and robbed and left on the side of the road. He spoke of how the Levite and priest passed him by, but a Samaritan took the time to stop and care for him. When Jesus turned to the one who was trying to trap Him and asked "and which one was the good neighbor?", I thought that that Scribe would just die. He had to answer: "the Samaritan." He had to admit that a so-called 'half-breed' whom the Pharisees and Scribes detested was a better neighbor than either the Levite or the priest. I could just hear my father telling such a story. He would have been delighted in passing such a story on. Jesus was merely telling in story form what my father lived. They both believed that what made a man good wasn't what he was or where he came from, but who he was and how that who was expressed in his actions.

Isn't it interesting how much of the Pharisee and Scribe can be found in all of us? We make judgment about someone, as they did about Jesus, and after that judgment has been made, we seem to find fault with everything that person says or does. Never mind the fact that one of our friends might say or do the same thing and we just pass it off.

As first I couldn't understand the attacks that were being made upon Jesus. Had these men not heard what Jesus was saying about a new order and a new kingdom? Couldn't they see that Jesus was the most refreshing and hopeful thing that had happened to our people? If this kingdom were to become a reality they would have to be won over. Jesus was certainly giving them every opportunity to see things in a new light. He had been patient yet firm in the manner in which He had answered their questions. He told the people to continue to listen to and respect these leaders. Despite all of this, they continued to ask questions and challenge Him.

It might seem to you at this point that I accepted everything Jesus had to say. Your assumption would be wrong. Some of Jesus' responses to the Pharisees' and Scribes' questions disturbed me, as did some of His philosophy regarding loving your enemies. One such question was put to Jesus, whether it was lawful to pay our taxes to Caesar or not. Knowing the answer they were looking for, I thought the question was hypocritical, since I knew that they scrupulously paid their taxes. And yet I was interested in hearing Jesus' answer to such a question. When Jesus responded that we should render to Caesar the things that are Caesar's and to God what is God's, I was not entirely pleased. But then I thought Jesus was merely trying to avoid starting the revolution before He was ready. As I reflect on it now, I still was hearing what I wanted to hear. I had rationalized away His answer.

What was really disturbing, and made me fearful about the coming of the kingdom was His sermon about loving your enemies. He was speaking about love and stated that it was easy to love those who love you. He said pagans did that. Then He said that we were called to a higher realm. When we speak of love in the higher realm, He said, it means loving all peoples, including your enemies. If He had stopped there, I could have learned to live with that. But He went on to say that to love your enemies means to learn to turn the other cheek and to do good to those who hurt us. Wait a minute! I thought. Did Jesus expect to kill the Romans with kindness? If so, I could assure Him He didn't know these Romans as I did. If this were His plan, I thought, His kingdom would never come about.

But even at this juncture, I hadn't given up hope about this kingdom of which He spoke. Time would teach Him that this part of His philosophy would not work. And this is why I was so angry with the Pharisees and Scribes. The Romans seemed to ignore Jesus. They saw Him, I thought, as just another one of a long line of prophets who never really amounted to much. As I strove to look at it through Jesus' eyes, I could see that He did not see the Romans as enemies. They, after all, left Him alone. The only people who seemed to be His adversaries were His own people. Although I did not realize it at this time, I would try to use this very confrontation between Jesus and our leaders to help Him see the Romans for what they really were.

To say that my relationship with Jesus and the eleven was growing more intimate by the day would not be an accurate statement. Any organization, if it is to become successful, must have within its structure what you might call the devil's advocate. This was someone who would point out another side of an impending decision. I was that someone. Jesus, I felt, was always on a different plane. It was His role to set forth the philosophy on which this new kingdom was to be based. It was the twelve, I thought, who had the responsibility to take this philosophy and make it practical. Now, you must understand that I loved the eleven. They were men with good hearts who would be willing to go the last mile for you. And they were never afraid of the work or the challenge set before them. But if I were to find fault with them, it would be that they were anything but practical. My friends were caught up with the emotions of the crowds we would encounter. They were caught up with the philosophy of Jesus. I finally came to realize that they acted always from the heart — not from the mind. I, on the other hand, rarely let my emotions run away with me. I was the only practical one in the group. I would have thought that at least Matthew, who had been a tax collector, would have seen the need to be practical in bringing about this kingdom. But even he and I would lock horns on some of the decision making.

These confrontations that took place between Jesus and the eleven on the one hand, and myself on the other, would not have ended our friendship. But I will say there were times when I felt I was wasting my breath. It was hard being the only one objecting to some of the decision making.

I began to feel that every time a decision was about to be made, the others would look at me to see what my objection would be. I sensed that, although they liked me, they had begun not to take me too seriously.

What were these confrontations about? They basically fell into two categories. The first category had to deal with money. Since I had been put in charge of the purse, I felt very strongly about how we used our treasury. The amount of money we had in the common purse came about because of the generosity of the people. Even though Jesus never spoke of money, people realized the cost of food and supplies and were somewhat generous. This is not to say that the purse was bulging with money, but it did help us a great deal with the expenses. The confrontation would come about when some one or some group would approach Jesus or one of the others with a cause or a sad story, and they would turn to me to dip into the purse to help these people. I did not object to helping the poor but they had to realize that we had our own expenses and (I kept this to myself) we needed to set aside some of our funds for the establishment of the kingdom. Our biggest confrontation came one evening when we were eating in a tax collector's house, and a woman came with very expensive aromatic oils and began to anoint Jesus' feet. I could not refrain from objecting. I told the rest that they always complained about my miserliness and here was this woman with this expensive oil, the purchase price of which could have gone to some of those with sad stories that were constantly coming to the eleven. After the eleven had just shaken their heads in disbelief, it was Jesus who vocalized His feelings. He said we should let her alone for she merely was preparing Him for His burial. I backed off, more because of Jesus' talk of death than the waste of money. This marked the third or fourth time Jesus alluded to His death as almost being imminent. Why on earth is He talking about His death, I thought. His talk disturbed me. But there were other things He was saying that disturbed me even more. And this leads to the second type of confrontation I had with Jesus and the eleven.

Before moving to our second point of confrontation, however, we should deal with how others thought about my holding the common purse. There were those who thought that the only reason I complained about spending money from the common purse was that if we didn't spend that money, I would have more money for myself. They thought I was taking money from the common purse, and they were correct. But my reason was not what they supposed. If Jesus and the eleven had had their way, they would have given away everything. Despite my objections, they continued to make an assault upon the purse with every sad story they heard. If we were to bring about this kingdom, some money would be needed to set it up. The money I was taking would be used for the kingdom.

The second type of confrontation came from Jesus' dealings with the Pharisees and Scribes. I have made mention of their attempt to trap Jesus by their questions and how Jesus was too clever for them. You would think they would have backed down. Instead they increased their efforts. As I stated before, I could not understand their actions. Up to this time, Jesus had handled them with great political astuteness. But eventually this began to change. It happened in the beginning ever so subtly. Jesus was asked for the millionth time why He spent so much time with sinners and tax collectors. He turned and with a smile on His face said "These people have need of healing and I am a physician." He could have stopped there but He chose to go further. "They admit their need for healing and therefore I can help them. You, on the other hand, I cannot help." Though it was subtly said, there was no doubt in Jesus' or their minds what He meant. The smiles on their faces remained, but you could tell that beyond the smile were clenched teeth. Even though Jesus had every right to make such a statement, even though He was correct in His assessment, this was not the way, I thought, to win these men over to our cause. If the kingdom was to come about, we would need these leaders to support us. And what began in subtlety was now becoming straightforwardness. When asked one day about the Pharisees and Scribes, Jesus told the people they should always respect their position, obey their rules, but never follow their examples. Perhaps Jesus felt that kind and gentle words had failed to win them over and that the only way to reach them now was to shock them, to force them to see themselves as they really were. If that was the case, I didn't think His way was working. My observations told me they were only getting more angry and determined to somehow stop Jesus.

When I brought my concerns to the eleven, I found that they too were concerned, but not for the same reasons. They felt that what Jesus had to say was all justified. They felt too that Jesus had never really acted to get even or to hurt His adversaries but rather had just been honest in answering their questions. They knew that Jesus never played games with people. With Him, you always knew where you stood. And so their concern wasn't about what Jesus had done but rather what might be done to Him. They weren't sure about His enemies. I agreed with the others' thoughts and concerns, and we decided to try to keep Jesus in a safe place and attempt, though none of us expected to be too successful, to ask Jesus to tone down His reflections. Although we agreed on our concern for Jesus' well-being, I seemed to be the only one concerned about the formation of the kingdom and our need to win over the Pharisees and Scribes. I kept these concerns to myself.

One other concern to which I alluded earlier was Jesus' preoccupation with going up to Jerusalem where He would suffer and die. When we approached Jesus about His confrontations with the Pharisees and Scribes, He responded, predictably, that He had to be true to Himself, reminding us again that we were on our way to Jerusalem where He would suffer and die. It was Peter, most often the spokesman for the twelve, who spoke up now, protesting that we would not permit such an event to happen. We knew Jesus was hurt at such a stand. We could see tears welling up in His eyes. He said "If I have taught you nothing else, I would have hoped that you would have learned to be true to yourself and what you are about. And here you stand asking me to compromise myself and thwart my mission, the very reason I was sent." With that, He went off from us to be alone.

The eleven accepted Jesus' slight chastisement and seemed in agreement to let Jesus be Himself and do what He needed to do. They feared for Him and what might happen but knew He had to be true to it all. I, on the other hand, was not quite ready to let go. Sensing the feelings of the rest, I knew I had to go this one alone. I knew I just needed time to think this one out.

If I was at fault in any of this, it was not because I didn't care. I did care, and not only about the establishment of the kingdom but also about Jesus and what would happen to Him. But as I reflect on it now, I know I was at fault. The fault lay not in the fact that I didn't care but that I still saw the kingdom as political and not spiritual. I was still hearing what I wanted to hear and not what Jesus was really saying. I wanted to be a prince in this new kingdom. Jesus wanted all men to be princes in His Father's kingdom. Jesus had asked us to take up our cross and follow after Him. He had asked us to lose control of our own lives and give them over to the Father as He was doing. I was willing to do as He had asked. I was willing to take up my cross. I had proven that by my three long years of service. Now I wanted my reward. I wanted to be a somebody in the kingdom. I was not about to turn myself over to the Father. I was not about to give up on my dream. I was not about to lose control of my destiny and life. But if I let Jesus do what He wanted — even if He would leave me alone — my dreams would be shattered. If I wanted my dream to become a reality, I not only needed full control of my own destiny, I needed control over Jesus' destiny as well. And so I did what all self-seeking individuals do, I began to rationalize. Jesus would be better off, if He would only begin to recognize the Romans as His enemies, mend fences with the

Pharisees and Scribes and establish a political kingdom here and now. Jesus, I thought, was lucky to have me amongst His friends. I was the only one who could orchestrate this. Later, He would thank me for taking control.

At this point I am sure you are looking at me and seeing a fool at work. But you have the advantage of knowing the outcome of my work. I did not have the same advantage. I hear some of you saying you would never have done what I did. But as I hear you saying this, I also remember Jesus saying "Let He who is without sin cast the first stone." You see, my friends, in many ways you are like me. You too hear the words of Jesus to take up your cross and follow Him. And you have answered as I did by working for the kingdom. But when Jesus explains that the cross is the symbolic action of losing control of your life and giving that control to the Father many of you do what I did. Most of us hate to lose control of any situation, let alone our lives. We need control of our lives if we are to make our dreams a reality. The sad thing is that we are shortsighted in our dreams. We think the short-term goals we have set will lead us to all that we ever wanted. I see that now in my own life. I thought if I only could get this political kingdom established, it would lead to all I ever wanted. But if I had been successful, I would have found I wanted more. For what I wanted—peace, security, fulfillment, happiness—could never be found in the establishment of a political kingdom. But had I been far-sighted I could have seen that all that I wanted was contained in the kingdom Jesus spoke of. And the cost, Jesus said, was the losing of control. But our problem is a lack of trust that the Lord knows what He is talking about. We are afraid that if we do what He asks, and it does not bring what we are looking for, then we have nothing. At least if we keep control, we can determine our own destiny. What we are saying then, although we would never vocalize it, is that we are smarter than the Lord. We have a better plan. And this was the fault that brought me to my next sequence of actions.

It was on a glorious Sunday that we entered Jerusalem. It was glorious because of the weather but even more glorious because of the thousands of people converging on Jesus. Some proclaimed Him to be their king. Others, by their waving of palms, proclaimed Him king by their actions. Now, maybe now, He would recognize His position and rightfully take the throne. Maybe now He would stop His foolish talk of death. Maybe now I would not have to come up with a plan to stem the tide. With such cheers of adulation, not even the Pharisees or Scribes could stop a coronation from taking place.

All my joyous expectations were short-lived. It seemed to me that He was doing everything He could to fulfill His prediction of death. It was on the third day of the week that He had gone to the temple and seen the money changers and merchants selling animals for sacrifice. Standing in the middle of the temple, He seemed to lose control. He grabbed a long rope that was on one of the tables and He began to use it as a whip, driving the animals from the outer courtyard. When He had finished doing that, He began to overturn all the tables, shouting as He did that His father's house was a house of prayer and they had made it a den of iniquity. These men were shocked. Many of them had been at the entrance of Jerusalem a few days before, declaring Jesus as their king. Jesus could not afford to make any more enemies and yet here He was doing what He could not afford to do. I knew I had to act, and act quickly.

But what could I do? What plan could be conceived that would reverse all that had happened?

The answer came the next day. I had been sent by the others to procure the items needed for the Passover Supper. As I moved among the shopkeepers and merchants at the market, I overheard people saying that the Pharisees and Scribes had put out a reward of thirty pieces of silver for anyone who could take the guards of the Sanhedrin to a quiet place where they might arrest Jesus. My first reaction was to think how horrible. But then I thought He had brought it upon Himself when He overreacted in the temple the day before.

I needed a quiet place to think and I knew the perfect spot. It is where Jesus and we twelve would go for a quiet time when we were in Jerusalem. I made my way a short distance to the garden of Gethsemane.

I sat on one of the rocks, trying to put all the factors together and come up with a plan. I needed to bring the Pharisees and Scribes together with Jesus. I needed to take advantage of Jesus' anger and direct it to the ones with whom He really should be angry: the Romans. And above all I needed to change His thoughts about an imminent death. I knew if I could get Jesus angry with the Romans, He would forget about dying. For if He would die (and the Romans were the only ones who by law could put Him to death) then it would mean that the Romans would win. I could not picture Jesus letting that happen. But how could I arrange a confrontation with the Romans? And then there was still the animosity between Jesus and the Pharisees and Scribes. And suddenly the answer came to me. Since I was having problems with three separate groups. I would merely pit all three against each other. And in the process I would earn 30 pieces of silver for the kingdom. I knew our leaders merely wanted to teach Jesus a lesson for what they would call His arrogance. They would take Him to Pilate to punish Him and that would be the end of it as far as they were concerned. I was just as sure, however, that once Jesus saw the Romans for what they really were. He would not speak of turning the other cheek as He had done before. And so I decided to let the Sanhedrin do my work for me, and I would get paid for doing it. And I point out to you, all this was done for the sake of the kingdom.

Isn't it strange that in our refusal to relinquish control of our own destiny, we demand that others relinquish their control to us? Here I was, painting this whole scenario, assuming each would play his part as I had written it. How about you? How often are you guilty of the same thing? And how angry do you get when the actors forget the lines you wrote for them? And of course our little play was written to benefit us all.

Certainly there was some risk in what I was about to do. And I had to admit that Jesus would experience some pain in this plan of mine. That was the part of the plan I did not like. But at this point in time I saw no way to avoid it. I felt for Him, but, in a way, He had caused much of what was to happen to Him. I knew, too, that others would not understand my plan. For that reason I had no intention of telling anyone until it was all over. Then they would understand and be grateful.

Looking back at what I have said, I sound so self-righteous. Here I was, in one breath saying I was sorry that Jesus was going to have to endure some pain due to my plan, and in the next breath saying it was His own fault. How many times do we blame someone else when what we do causes pain or hurt? We have such a hard time accepting responsibility for our actions.

I started toward the Sanhedrin, making my way down the crowded little streets, having decided that a quiet place where Jesus could be handed over was the garden I had just left. I was sure that this would be the place where Jesus would want to go after the Passover Supper. The eleven would be there with Him but that couldn't be helped. They would just have to understand. My thought was that if the Sanhedrin guards would be great in number, the eleven would not be foolish enough to defend Jesus. I marked that thought down in my head for when I finalized plans with the Sanhedrin.

When I arrived at the Sanhedrin and explained my purpose at the gate, I was immediately ushered into Annas' huge chambers. Several of the others were present when I said I would be willing to lead them to a quiet spot where Jesus would be. I told them of their need to have many guards because Jesus would be accompanied there by his small band of followers. One of the members said he was glad His followers would be there; they too could be arrested. I panicked. This was not the way the plan was to go. I interjected that this would create unnecessary problems for the Sanhedrin. The followers, I assured them, would panic and scatter. Without Jesus, I said, they would be leaderless. They agreed.

They then wanted to get down to the details of the handing over: when and where was it to take place? Before I would set the details, I said, I had to know what they planned to do with Jesus. Annas merely smiled and said that their only interest was to teach this arrogant Jesus a lesson. But he added that the lesson must be public so that others like Him would learn the lesson as well. For that reason it was necessary to take Him to Pilate. It was, at this point, going as planned. But I wanted an out in case things changed. I told them that it would be the night of Passover. I lied and said I was not sure of the place but would come here to get them. They agreed and told me I would be paid when the deed was done.

With mixed emotions, I left Annas' house. Had I done the right thing? Would this go as planned? Would Jesus and the eleven understand that this was not personal? I was glad I had left myself an out by not sharing the location of the event. I was glad that the meal was only hours away. The preparation and the actual meal would be time-consuming and not leave me much time to reconsider what I had just done. These were the questions and thoughts that ran through the back of my mind as I made my way to the upper room.

As I entered, I saw several of my companions huddled in the corner of the room. They motioned for me to join them. As I made my way to them, I saw how tense and shaken they were. Before I even reached them, Andrew blurted out "Have you heard the rumor that they have put a price on His head?" I nodded that I had heard. It was Matthew who asked "What are we going to do?" They all began to speak at the same time. It seemed that all of them agreed that at least tonight Jesus would be safe here in the upper room and later in the garden. It would give them time to figure a way to get Jesus away from Jerusalem tomorrow. It was obvious they had not known the Sanhedrin's entire plan. They did not know that the Sanhedrin was looking for a quiet spot like the garden to arrest Him. Their anxiety now made me think of my actions.

Our conversation became quiet as Jesus walked into the room. What was I going to do now? I could not share my thoughts with them. They would be shocked. They would never understand. Grave doubts now entered my thinking. Maybe they were right. Maybe, if we could get through this night, we could get Jesus away from Jerusalem tomorrow. But even if we did, we would merely be postponing the inevitable. The real solution was to get Jesus to change His attitude toward His adversaries. I would see if this were possible. I would approach Him and tell Him of the rumor. I would wait for His reaction and see if He would seek my advice.

My stomach churned as I approached Him. He remarked on the beautiful day and said He had decided to take a walk with Peter and John. When He finally looked into my eyes, He saw how tense I was. He asked what was wrong. I asked in return if

He had heard anything on His walk through the streets. No, He said, nothing too earth-shattering. I then told Him of the rumor. I presented it to Him just as the others had shared it with me. His look told me that He hadn't heard but that He wasn't surprised. I asked Him if there was something that I could do. With a sad and tired smile, He asked, "Haven't you already done it?" I was at one and the same time shocked, embarrassed, sick, hurt and puzzled. I asked what He meant. He told me in a quiet tone that on His walk today, He had seen me coming from Annas' house. He had wondered why I had been there, but now He knew. He told me I didn't have to worry, John and Peter had stopped to talk with one of the merchants and had not seen me. I couldn't look at Him. My hands shook. I turned and sought the door. I needed air. He knew and there was nothing I could do now but go through with it.

The hours of preparation of the Passover Meal now lay heavy on me. I wanted this night to be over.

Finally the time for the meal came. I could not believe how excited Jesus was. He told us how much He had been looking forward to celebrating this Passover with us. He could see how anxious I was. I began to tremble when He spoke of betrayal. We looked at one another. The eleven were wondering what He meant while I was wondering whether they would figure it out. Jesus motioned for me and whispered that it probably was time for me to go and do what I had to do. He did it in such a way that the others thought He was just sending me on an errand. My nausea returned.

As I made my way to the Sanhedrin, I had to stop every few yards to take a deep breath. I felt dizzy and weak. The sooner my part in all this was over, the better.

I finally arrived at Annas' house. They were waiting for me. I told them Jesus could be found in the Garden of Gethsemane. They told me that I had to accompany them to the Garden and point this Jesus out. I protested that my part of the bargain had been completed. The guards then grabbed me and dragged me with them. I thought, as we made our way, that I didn't have the courage to face Jesus — especially with the others there.

As I reflect on it now, I think how foolish and stupid I

was to have put Jesus, the eleven, and myself through all of this. I had had so many warnings to stop this whole affair. I should have listened in the beginning to the wisdom of the eleven when they determined to let Jesus do what He had to do. How many times have you failed to listen to the wisdom of your friends and gone ahead with your own ill-conceived plan?

When I was in the Garden on that fateful afternoon and conceived of this plan, why didn't I at least listen to my own doubts? Was I so sure that this was the thing to do? If I wasn't sure myself, why did I go forward with it? And when I left an out for myself by not identifying the place, didn't I realize that now was the time to stop all of this? How often have you had real doubts about what you were planning to do, and gone ahead with your actions despite those doubts?

And then when Jesus, with a sigh, told me He knew what I was going to do, why then did I assume I had to go through with it? How often have you acted even when you knew beyond any shadow of a doubt that what you were about to do was wrong?

And finally, the fact that I was ashamed to perform this action in front of Jesus and the eleven should have told me that I must stop this before it went any further. How many times have you, despite the fact you felt ashamed, felt compelled to finish what you had started? Why did you feel compelled? If I could have answered that question for myself, maybe I would have stopped and refused to go any further. Unfortunately I didn't stop.

When we reached the Garden, I thought I would be able to take the cowardly way out. I thought I could avoid the embarrassment by pointing Jesus out from the back of the crowd. But they wanted to embarrass me as much as they thought they would embarrass Him. They obviously didn't know Jesus as I knew Him. He would not be embarrassed but He would be deeply hurt. They told me I was to go and embrace this Jesus, so they could be sure they were arresting the right man. They knew who Jesus was. They just wanted to make sure that there was no doubt who had been bought by thirty pieces of silver.

Shaking and with tears rolling down my face, I stepped forward and embraced Jesus. With a look of hurt and betrayal upon His face, He put His arms around me and merely said, "Judas, Judas." I had no time to respond, as they immediately stepped forward and grabbed Him. Even if I had had time, I don't know what I would have said to Him.

As they came forward to grab Him, one of the Pharisees, in front of the shocked eleven, handed me a bag filled with the thirty pieces of silver. I looked around at the faces of the eleven. Their look told me they couldn't believe their eyes. I ran from the Garden.

I ran till I could run no longer. I stopped, to catch my breath and to collect my thoughts. I had done it. I had betrayed Him. But wait, I thought. I had done this for the kingdom. I did not realize how hard this was going to be, but the plan was still intact. Please God, I prayed, make the plan work! If it didn't, I didn't know what I was going to do.

I made my way back to Annas' house, knowing that was where they would surely take Jesus. By the time I got there they had already taken Jesus inside. I noticed that the servants and a rather huge crowd were around the back of the house, and so I decided to stay toward the front, in the shadows. I was still shaking but much less than I had been before. I was starting to calm down. Everything would work out. The plan was still intact. I pushed from my mind thoughts of how Jesus and the eleven were taking the events that had just transpired. I didn't want to think of what they thought of me. I had done what I had done. The hope of justification now lay in the unfolding of the plan. If it worked, the past could be set aside. Please God, let it work, I thought.

It was getting later and later. I wondered why it was taking so long. I came out of the shadows and walked around the building. I spotted John and Peter there. They didn't see me. I had no desire to encounter them. It would, I thought, just end up in a confrontation, a confrontation that I was not ready for. I had just begun to regain my confidence in the plan I had orchestrated. I had begun to get control of my emotions. Because they had chastised me in the past for some of the things I had said and done, I was sure that they would have written me off as insane or worse—greedy. And I didn't need that now. The problem was, as I said before, they always acted from the heart. I, for the most part, acted from the mind. They could never see the intelligence at work and the strategy working just as I had planned it. After my plan had completely unfolded before their eyes, they would be thanking me for my bold move. They would then see me in a different light. No longer would they think me insane or greedy, but rather, a genius.

What about you? Are you like Peter and John who always acted from their heart, or more like me who always had everything calculated and planned out? What Peter, John and I forgot was that the Lord gave each of us a mind and a heart, fully expecting that we would act with both. Peter's and John's acting from the heart and me solely from the intellect eventually got the three of us in trouble. The emotions help temper the intellect and make us consider the ramifications of our actions for all involved. The intellect tempers the emotions and helps us see what is possible and reasonable. The three of us needed to blend the two.

Anyway, I turned and walked back from where I had come. They were bringing Jesus out — with hands tied behind His back. Such a scene could only mean one thing: they were taking Him to Pilate. All was going as planned.

I knew those hours before the Sanhedrin had been hard on Jesus. But He had been rebuffed and ostracized by some of our leaders before. He had been scarred but had always emerged a stronger man. I did not want Him to have to endure such treatment at the hands of His own people but, as I said before, I did not know any other way to get Him brought before that infidel Pilate and his cohorts. I knew no other way to shake His very foundation and force Him to realize His way would never work. I could feel His pain and humiliation, but I also felt that in the end He would thank me. I felt I was back on track and everything was going to be all right.

Why is it that we always think our way is better? Why is it that we don't have a problem when someone else needs to learn a lesson (sometimes the hard way) but we are offended when someone tries to teach us a lesson?

They brought Him to Pilate and Pilate took Him inside his chambers. It seemed like days, not hours, before Pilate had emerged. He stood there amongst his bodyguards. Jesus was nowhere to be found. I began to worry. Where was He? What had they done with Him? I felt my emotions were running away with me. One moment everything was all right, the next moment I was overcome with panic.

When the crowd began to quiet down, Pilate addressed them. He reminded them that it was his custom at the time of the feast of Passover to release to them one of his prisoners. At this point, he turned and nodded to one of the guards and they brought forward a rather huge and muscular man named Barabbas. Behind him came Jesus. My heart almost stopped beating, and tears filled my eyes. This was not the Jesus who, a few hours before, had been taken to Pilate's chambers. This was a Jesus cloaked in a robe, bent over in pain, and wearing a crown of thorns. I could see, where the cloak did not cover the body, parts of the flesh gouged away by the awful scourging that had taken place. Blood trickled down His face from the thorns that invaded His head.

I wanted His foundation shaken but must it have gone this far? I found myself sobbing. Had I miscalculated? Had I made a mistake? Lest I lose my grip on reality, my thoughts jumped back to the week before. It was the night before He triumphantly entered Jerusalem for the last time. He stood on a high hill and wept. He spoke of the destruction that Jerusalem would eventually endure. He cried out in anguish, saying, "If only they had listened!" As I wept at the sight of a broken man, I cried, "If only He had listened."

Isn't it strange when someone doesn't agree with us or doesn't understand us, we assume that they are not listening, but when someone accuses us of not listening, we are offended?

I began to be flooded with doubts. Maybe I was wrong. Maybe I had gone too far. My heart was racing far ahead of my mind. I had to stop, take a deep breath and let my mind catch up with my heart. I began first by turning my back on Jesus. As long as my eyes focused on my beaten friend, I could not collect my feelings. I needed time to stop and think — to get a hold on my emotions. You see, my emotions were trying to temper my intellect, and I wouldn't let that happen. (Why is it that so many of us are afraid of our emotions?) As I took a moment to pull myself together, I began to reflect on the events of the moment. All was not lost. Two things, I was sure, would now happen. Jesus would finally come to realize that you cannot turn your cheek to your enemies. You cannot win over infidels like these Romans with pacifism. You can only win them over with might. Jesus had had to pay a great price to learn that lesson but learn it I'm sure He had.

The second thing I was sure would happen was that once my people saw how broken and pathetic Jesus looked they would demand His release. After all, Barabbas was known to be a murderer and cutthroat. They would not want him back on the streets of Jerusalem. As far as Jesus was concerned, I was sure that all the Sanhedrin wanted was for Jesus to be taught a lesson. I was sure that the physical evidence of His brokenness would be enough for them to realize that the lesson had been taught.

My mind had caught up with and regained control of my emotions and my heart. I began to turn around, mumbling under my breath, "All is not lost — all is not lost."

I heard Pilate giving the people their options. He ended his address with the words "and whom do you wish me to release — Barabbas or this Jesus of Nazareth?" I shouted in a loud voice, "Jesus of Nazareth!" but I was drowned out by the booming voices that sounded as one: "Release to us Barabbas!" I could not believe my ears! This was not the way it was to happen. Jesus was not the enemy, the Romans were. Jesus was our hope. He just needed to get a few things straightened in His own mind and He would be all right. I was sure His experience with the guards had gone a long way in helping Him sort out the manner in in which to deal with the Romans. I pushed through the crowd, shouting, "No, no, release Jesus! He is our only hope!" It was my futile attempt to get the people to think about what they were doing. I say futile only because it caused them to shout all the louder, "Release to us Barabbas!"

When things began to calm down amongst the crowd, I heard Pilate ask, "What, then, would you have me do with

Jesus?" "That's it, that's it!" I found myself screaming from within. "Make them stop and think what this all means. Let them see that this is not the road to take." But the people never stopped to think what they were doing. They didn't take advantage of a second chance that Pilate was giving them. Instead they shouted "Crucify Him! Crucify Him!" "What, wait," I shouted, "you don't know what you're doing." The louder I shouted the louder they screamed "Crucify Him! Crucify Him!"

When the crowd had finally calmed down, Pilate stood there, looking confused. "Why?" he said incredulously. "What has He done to deserve death?" 'Precisely,' I thought. I couldn't believe it. I was agreeing with this infidel Pilate. I was taking his side over my own people. This was the third time he'd given them a chance to change their minds. They just shouted the louder, "Crucify Him! Crucify Him!" And then added the crushing blow: "If you don't, we'll tell Caesar!"

The people had gotten lost in their emotions. Three times they were given the opportunity to stop and think about what they were doing. Three times they let their emotions run away with them. Does this ever happen to you?

The die was cast. Pilate had gone as far as he could. I felt sorry for him. He had tried but he could not stem the tide. And I thought the Zealots had taught me to hate "them," meaning the Romans, to see "them" as infidels who had come to invade "my" people's land, to take away "our" greatness. And there I was, feeling sorry for one of "them". I questioned my feelings, but just for a moment. I quickly realized that at least he had taken the time to think things out. At least he'd tried to do the right thing. That was far more than "my" people had done. And I began to wonder about other things I had been carefully taught. Here I was, priding myself on how intelligent I was, how I always acted from my mind and never from my heart. I had never taken the time to discern between the good I was taught and the application of that good when it came to others. Everything had been black and white to me. All my life I had seen only one road that lay ahead and I courageously took it. All my life I had divided people into two groups, those who were on the right road and those who weren't. That was my past. But here in the present stood a man who moments ago I had called an infidel.

Here stood a man who definitely was on a different road than I, and yet I found it hard to judge him badly. I struggled in that moment to see into the future, to see if these two uniquely different roads could not somehow merge. I was prevented from seeing that far ahead. Without conclusive evidence of such a merger, my previous self would have judged him to be on the wrong road. But now I wasn't so sure. Things were no longer black and white for me. Others no longer fell into another camp just because they didn't seem to be on the same road.

What about you? Do you see things as being black and white? Are you able to see any gray area in your life or in others'? Do you tend to make judgment, as I did about Pilate, without really knowing the person or the situation? Do you tend to make judgment due to what a person is and not who he is? I had judged Pilate before solely on the fact he was a Roman governor — the *what* that he was — instead of the fact that he was a caring and thinking person — the *who* that he was.

My life now was a total shambles. My plan, which I had perceived as brilliant, was nothing more than the stupid act of a proud man who thought he knew more than his Messiah and best friend.

I still foolishly thought that "all was not lost." Even though my plan was a shambles, I still had hope for Jesus. My hope was not that Jesus would come to see these Romans as His enemies, but that He somehow would be able to avoid any more suffering and humiliation.

My first hope for this was that Jesus would be able to do what He had done in the past. There had been other times when others had decided that He must die and He somehow miraculously walked away. Since I felt responsible for what was transpiring, I decided to follow the cross-bearing Jesus through the streets. I had hoped to see His miraculous walk once again. I saw Him fall once and then a second time. My heart was pounding and tears rolled down my face. It was my fault. It was my fault. When was He going to walk away from all of this — and if He wasn't, why was He struggling to get up with each fall? I began to scream within myself. "No more! No more! Stay down! Stay down!"

When He fell the second time, I saw Him struggle to get up. He did it in a way that told me that this strong-willed individual was determined to finish what had begun. He had told us before arriving in Jerusalem, that while here He would be arrested and would die upon the cross. He was determined to complete what He had predicted. There would be no walking away on His part. There would be no dying in the streets. He was determined to make it to Golgotha.

Even so, I still had not given up hope that this could all be stopped. You see, I had not given up the notion that I still had some control over what was to happen. As I reflect on it now, the key word here was the word control. I remember Jesus often saying He had come to do the will of His Father. It was of late that in the same context He spoke of going to Jerusalem where He said He would be arrested and die. I never stopped to realize that His death might have something to do with His Father's will. I never stopped to realize it because it was not the plan I had in mind. And now, even though Jesus was determined to make it to Golgotha, I was just as determined to see to it that He didn't.

My last resort was to go to the Sanhedrin. There were only a few of the members at Annas' house. The rest, no doubt, were on their way to Golgotha to see to it that they finally would be rid of this so-called "Messiah." Those who stayed behind were somewhat startled as I pushed my way past the servants and into the chamber where they were. "I want this whole affair to end now." I said. "Here, here are your thirty pieces of silver." As I said this, I threw the pieces on the table. They laughed at me. They asked me if I didn't realize that it was better for one man to die for the sake of all.

One of them took the small sack, replaced the coins in it and handed it back to me. He said, "What's done is done." My heart sank. I could not change what I had done — Jesus was going to die.

At that instant the servants burst into the room and grabbed me. I pulled loose for a moment — just enough time to throw the coins on the floor. I shouted, as much for myself as for them, that I hadn't thought it would go this far. They smiled and said, "What is that to us? You should have known." The next thing I knew, I was being thrown out on the street with the sound of the servants' laughter ringing in my ears.

I was lost. I had no more options left — no more control. It's only now that I realize I never really had much control in the first place. The only real control I had had was in the choice of my own actions. I had had the option of pointing Jesus out or not. The actions of the Sanhedrin, Pilate, and Jesus were all up to them. Those actions were their choices.

The little control I'd had, I had lost. I had no more plans. I found myself muttering under my breath, "All is now lost."

I felt lost and alone. Everyone would know what I had done but no one would ever realize why I had done it. If all had gone as planned, everyone would have understood my actions. Now that all had gone awry, they would count me as just a greedy man who found Jesus of little use to himself anymore.

They just had to understand that this was not the case. They just had to understand I had a plan that would have benefited us all. I must tell them. They had to believe me.

I thought back to when I was following Jesus. I could recall seeing only John following with Mary. Where were the others? The only place that they might be was the upper room where we had eaten the night before. I made my way there. I needed to talk to them. I needed them to understand. I needed to tell them of my plan. I needed to tell them that this proud and arrogant man was sorry for all that had happened.

I tapped lightly on the door. It was James who opened the door a crack. When he saw it was I, he opened the door and let me in.

Once in, I could not contain myself. I told them that this was not supposed to be the way it was. To explain, I blurted out my plan. I admitted how proud and arrogant I had been. By now tears were flowing freely down my face. I looked at the faces of the others for understanding and was somewhat surprised at what I saw. Almost to a man, there was an ever-so-slight smile and a shaking of the head. It was almost as if they were saying, "Judas, Judas, how foolish you were to think you could have manipulated Jesus." It was Peter who, himself teary-eyed, came and embraced me. "It's all right," he said, "It's all right." Then, one by one, each came. Some embraced me — others just patted me on the arm. There was a great somberness in the room. Then, beginning with Peter, each confessed how they too had failed Jesus. Each in his own way had said we all had been guilty in regard to our friendship with Him. They were telling me they understood. They were telling me they forgave me. But I, in my frenzied state of mind, did not at that point hear their words of understanding, did not hear their words of forgiveness. All I could see and hear were ten men broken and shattered by what they had done. Instead of letting their words of understanding and forgiveness touch and heal my heart, I took their brokenness and guilt upon myself. Had I not pointed Jesus out, I thought, they never would have been put into a situation of denial or flight. I not only was guilty of Jesus' innocent blood, I was also guilty of breaking the others down to the point where they were now. I could not accept their forgiveness or even that of Jesus — if I thought He would give it — because I could not find it in my heart to forgive myself.

At least now others understood why I had done what I had done. To me that was the important thing. Now there was left but one thing to do. I had to be free of this burden, this guilt. I grabbed some rope from the upper room and found the closest tree.

— — — — — —

I began this story by saying that it might seem strange to have my story in a book entitled *Conversion Road* along with people like Peter and John. I hope that having heard my story you will now realize that like Peter and John and the rest, I traveled down Conversion Road with Jesus. The only difference was that I didn't have the courage to finish the journey with Him as they did.

My reason for wanting to share with you my journey down Conversion Road was twofold. My *primary reason* was the hope that you would learn from my mistakes.

My first mistake was my failure to realize that my true value lay in who I was and not in what I was or what I had. My wise father tried to teach me that lesson in my youth. Jesus tried to teach me that lesson in my adult years. In my stubbornness, I set aside the wisdom of these men and adopted instead the so-called wisdom of the world which stated that your net worth came from what you possessed. The world said that value came from without; my father and Jesus said that true value came from within. I wished I had listened to my father and Jesus. I hope you don't have to experience what I experienced before you learn this lesson.

My second mistake was my failure to realize that God's will for me is my happiness. Because I failed to realize that fact, I felt I needed to maintain control over my life. My happiness, I thought, lay solely in what I said and did. If that were the case, I thought, I could never cede control of my life to God. The ramifications to this way of thinking were many. Due to this faulty way of thinking, I had to rely on my own intelligence over any wisdom that would come from others. The wisdom of others might sway me and thus I might lose control. I also came to realize that if my dreams were to come to pass, I not only needed control of my own life, I needed control over others' lives as well. As a result of this, I not only failed to recognize the far-sighted wisdom of Jesus, but even tried to control His life to achieve my dream. This led to my arrogant thought that I was smarter than the Lord. If you could only come to realize and believe that God's will is our happiness, you could avoid all these ramifications. To cede your will to the Lord's is the assurance of your happiness. He wants for you what you want.

My third failure was that I heard what I wanted to hear and not what was really being said. I had such a desire to be someone of importance in a political kingdom, that I failed to hear that Jesus was not speaking of a political kingdom but a spiritual one. Had I heard what Jesus was really saying, I don't know whether I would have chosen to continue my pursuit of a kingdom that was merely spiritual or not. But had I heard what Jesus was really saying, I know I wouldn't have fallen into my current dilemma. Strive always to hear what is really being said, and it will help you avoid many false assumptions and many roads leading to dead ends.

My fourth failure was in assuming that emotions just get in your way. As I shared before, I prided myself on always acting from the mind. I found fault with the eleven because I always felt they acted solely from the heart. From reading my story, you might conclude that I was right about my emotions. It seems that those emotions led me to find the closest tree. But if the fact be known, it was my failure to integrate my mind with my heart that led me to that tree. It was the same fact that led the eleven to their denial and flight. As I said before, the Lord gave us both the heart and the intellect. He fully expected us to use both when acting. The emotions help temper the intellect and make us consider the ramifications of our actions on others. The intellect tempers the emotions and helps us see what is possible and reasonable. Never be afraid of your emotions but never act solely from them. Use both the mind and the heart and you can't go too far wrong.

The *secondary reason* I wanted to share my story with you was that you would realize why I did what I did. History has not treated me well. It is easy for those who look at history to judge from externals. I know. I judged Pilate and the Roman government by their external actions. It is important that you know why I acted as I did so that in judging your brothers and sisters you might look beyond mere externals to get at the root of the action — the answer to the question Why.

I am fully aware that what I did was wrong. Having done what I did, the only regret that I had before looking for that tree was that I did not go in search of Jesus first. Had I found Him I would have had no use for the rope or the tree. The burden would have been lifted from my back and I would have been healed. Know that no matter what you do, His love is the only force you need for healing. You merely have to seek it.

I hope my story has helped you on your journey down Conversion Road. Having heard of the many dead-end streets that I took might help you avoid the same wrong turns. Do as Jesus asked — take up your cross and follow Him, and remember the Father's will for you is your happiness.